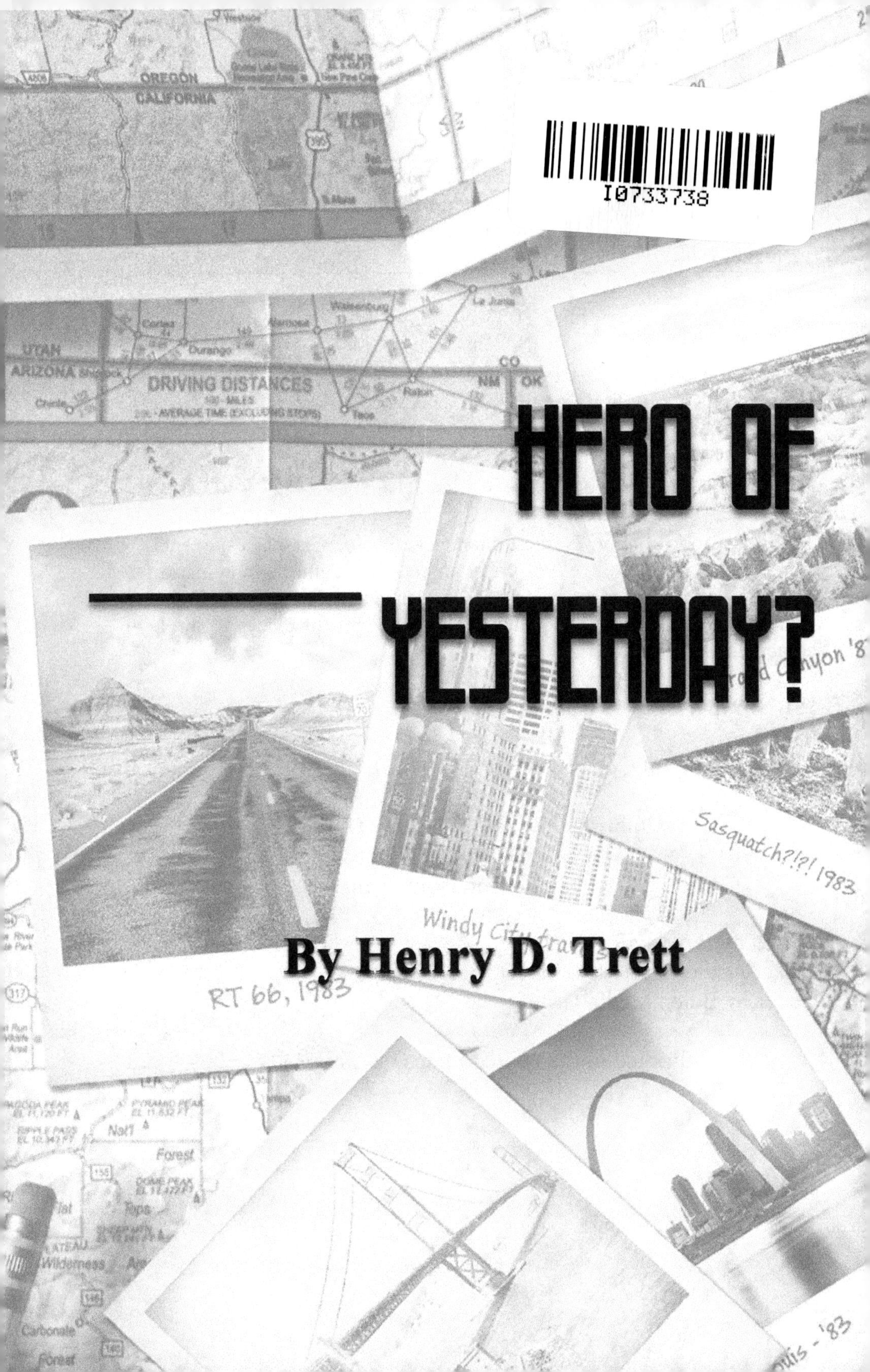
I0733738
HERO OF YESTERDAY?
By Henry D. Trett
DRIVING DISTANCES
OREGON
CALIFORNIA
UTAH
ARIZONA
Sasquatch?!?! 1983
Windy City
RT 66, 1983

Sale of this book without a front cover may be unauthorized. If this book is coverless, it may have been reported to the publisher as "**unsold** or **destroyed**" and neither the author nor the publisher may have received payment for it.

Copyright © 2023 by Henry D. Trett

All rights reserved. No portion of this book may be reproduced in any form without permission from the publisher except as permitted by U.S. copyright law.

For permission, contact **Belen Books, LLC**.

This is a work of fiction. Names, characters, businesses, places, events, locales, and incidents are either the products of the author's imagination or used in a fictitious manner. Any resemblance to actual persons, living or dead, the meandering sasquatch, or actual events or places is purely coincidental.

ISBN: 978-1-959715-15-3

Library of Congress Control Number: **2023931736**

Published by **Belen Books, LLC**
7901 4th St. N, Ste 300, St. Petersburg, FL. 33702 USA
Belenbookspublishing.com

Edited by Beverly R. Waalewyn
Jacket Author Photo by Gilbert Joel Velasquez
Cover by Belen Media Group

Printed in the United States of America
38°16'24.0"N 108°08'32.0"W

For M.E.

Yesterday is not ours to recover, but tomorrow is ours to win or lose.

—Lyndon B Johnson

"I don't blame you for writing of me as you have. You had to believe other stories, but then I don't know if anyone would believe anything good of me anyway."

—Billy the Kid

HERO OF _____ YESTERDAY?

My Editor is an Asshole

A Preface of Sorts

Okay, so at this point, I should make note that my editor said I needed to recap my story to where we are now. I, of course, protested this request. Yet, she said, "Some people may not have heard of your story before…."

"So, where in the hell have they been for the last five years, living under a rock in Wyoming?" I asked.

She answered, "Maybe… maybe not, but you must assume that people reading this book have never heard of you."

I laughed, "*What?* You can't be serious."

"No, I'm being serious," she said, "It's quite possible that somebody out there has not heard of, or read about, your story before."

"How is that possible? I did one of the most controversial things ever, and in the social media age, how could somebody have missed that?"

But my editor was insistent about this recap, so I countered: "What will you do if I don't do it?"

"You want your second book published, right?" she responded dryly.

"Of course."

"Then do the fucking recap!" was her final words, and that was that.

We went back and forth for a while over this topic, but we eventually settled upon an accord. Yes, I would write the fucking recap, as requested, but I would retain sole control over the chapter title. So, without further ado, I bid you welcome to the Chapter titled: *"My Editor is an Asshole."*

So, for those of you who somehow missed it…

Hello, my name is David Alan Taylor, a white male, mostly content with the solitude that came with a life of anonymity. I'm sure you have heard everything about me and what I did. My editor, however, has some reservations about your intellect and ability to remember anything you've read or seen.

Hero of the Yesterday?

Yes, it was in all the papers, on all the TV networks, and brought to you in real time by the trolls on the web. So, I'm sure you have heard the sordid details of my life from those who know me, those who think they know me, and so many of those trying to cash in on my misfortune.

Yet, for those who may have somehow overlooked it, I shot and killed four young black men on my 30th birthday in the streets of Orlando. A fifth person, Theo Roberts, survived, paralyzed from the waist down. Now, to be fair, they did rob and beat the shit out of some poor unfortunate soul before our chance encounter.

And Curtis Jones, my first 'victim' as some people liked to call him, shot an Orlando Police Officer in the back. It is important to note that I was not armed at this point; it was, after all, the fallen Officer's gun that I would use when things went sideways. But, regardless, I did pull the trigger and fire a bullet into the head of Curtis Jones.

By this point, things had passed the point of no return. More shots were fired, and more people died. Those of us lucky enough to survive the initial encounter *literally* fought for our lives. And in the background, I could hear someone very close to me begging, *"Please, don't die. Please don't die."*

Spoiler alert, I didn't die. So, with the help of my best friend, Terry, and supported by a highly complex relationship with a girl named Robyn, I reached the other side of this public relations cluster-fuck. Add in a long-lost daughter named Stacey and an elite lawyer named Alice Miller, and you get even closer to what happened. Finally, just for good measure, mix in a beautiful reporter named Traci Kaneko and an antagonist named Dr. James Johnson, then you get a better idea of what I experienced.

Eventually, it went to trial, and I was acquitted in the criminal case. However, in its infinite wisdom, another court found me guilty of civil violations of the dead, producing a financial penalty that resulted in a significant amount of money. I should continue to fight this verdict in court, but time was never on my side. So, there you have it; the basis of my notoriety is rooted in the counterculture revolution of our laws.

For some odd reason, I am what you would call a polarizing figure. People either love or hate me; there doesn't seem to be a whole lot of middle ground for someone who has done what I have done. I hope that, in time, people will understand that I am not the asshole of this story. Well, not the biggest asshole, anyways. But time, however fleeting, is the only currency that really matters. And you, my dear reader, have much less time than you ever imagined.

So, I would strongly recommend that you read the first book, but hey, I can't tell you what to do. Try to catch up or flounder in your ignorance; the choice is yours to make. And yes, I see the humor in your dilemma. But truth be told, after all, that I've been through, I don't give a damn.

I'm Back!

For better or worse, I've come back with another story to tell. I know, I know, I didn't think I'd ever be here either, yet here I am. And if I'm being completely honest, I was perfectly happy with the life I had cultivated ever since *the incident*. As far as I was concerned, another book wasn't necessary. So then, the question for you, the reader, becomes, what happened to change that?

A tragic event occurred not long ago, leading me to reconsider what I understood to be true about this life. The aftermath of this event left me with an incredible story that just needed to be shared with the rest of the world. As a result, and against my better judgment, I wrote another book, two more, actually. Most people will overlook the essential part of the last sentence and, instead, focus on the 'two books' comments. But a curious person would ask: *'Against my better judgment,'* what, exactly, does that mean?

I don't know how to tell you this without sounding like an alarmist, but the truth is no longer relevant; only opinions matter now. And for me, at least, that is a very frightening thought. This seismic shift in civility and discourse over the last few years has pushed me into quiet acceptance of the new reality encompassing our lives, but recent events have me questioning that logic.

Yes, I had discovered it's dangerous to hold an opinion that runs contrary to the majority. Yes, the winds of public opinion whipsaw back and forth across the serrated edge of insanity; and they do so without mercy for those who end up on the wrong side of that imaginary line drawn in the sand. Yet, I have no idea who is responsible for this debacle, but I'd like to think that we, as a society, can fix this predicament.

Of course, some people like Theo Roberts could accept what had happened without blaming me for the world's inequities. It was an odd friendship, considering how we met. I mean, we tried to kill each other that first night. The truth is, if Theo were a better shot, then I'd be dead, and none of this would have mattered. But as it is, I now walk with a slight limp, and Theo is paralyzed from the waist down.

I once asked Theo, "If you could do it all over again, would you change anything?"

"I wouldn't have pulled the trigger."

"Then I would have shot you, most likely killed you," I replied.

Theo reminded me, "You *did* shoot me."

I chuckled, "Not on purpose. I hit the ground, and the gun went off. It could have been you, anybody, or even nobody. It was just dumb luck."

Theo replied, "It took a little time for me to accept that it was truly God's will. You and me, David, are destined to do good for this Earth. There can be no other reason why we survived; others would die so young, with so much life to live."

And, of course, there were people like Dr. James Johnson who could not accept what had happened without blaming me for the inequities of this world. After publishing my first book, I discovered Dr. Johnson was in New York City. As a joke, I invited him to dinner; much to my surprise, he accepted.

It was an odd dinner, considering how we met. I mean, metaphorically speaking, we tried to kill each other in the court of public opinion. The truth is, if he were just a little bit sharper with his argument, then I'd be forgotten, and none of this would have mattered. But as it was, I got famous, and Dr. Johnson got rich.

After dinner, while sharing an expensive bottle of Bordeaux, I asked Dr. Johnson, "If you could do it all over again, would you change anything?"

"I would have come at you harder."

I asked, "Harder? How? Why?"

"Because you are a better man than I thought," he plied.

Confused, I answered, "I'm not sure what you mean?"

"When I first saw you," the doctor responded professionally. "I thought crucifying you with a public opinion would be easy. I was wrong. I had no idea how much fight and heart you held inside that broken body of yours, but there is only so much life left to live; it would be mendacious of me not to acknowledge my enjoyment of our theoretical differences. Perhaps, people like you and I, David, are destined to do something in this world.

"Perhaps, people like you and I, David, are the key to finally bridging the abyss that divides one side from the other."

My Thoughts on the Subject at Hand

Nobody gives a damn, but I would like to share my thoughts on the subject. It has been my experience that we are all more alike than anyone would care to admit. We all struggle to establish order in a world that thrives on chaos. We all love our family, friends, and sense of community, even if we don't say it often enough to the people who mean the most to us. We all dream of a better tomorrow while fighting the unyielding demands of today. We live, we laugh, and we cry. We have hopes, we have successes, and we have failures. Ultimately, we all seek our versions of *Truth*, *Justice*, and *The American way*.

And people wonder why it is so maddening to me that we don't recognize these similarities in one another. We focus on the differences; we wax nostalgic about the petty things that keep us apart. Our attention is drawn to the variations in skin color, hair, and clothes, which only serve to obscure our humanity. We are the problem, and ironically enough, we are also the solution. And if we can't see that in one another, perhaps we don't deserve the clarity we claim to seek.

According to the general scientific consensus, the Earth has existed for 4.5 billion years. Some 240 million years ago, dinosaurs began ascending, resulting in a reign that lasted 174 million years. 'Modern Man' arrived late to the party, branching off from our distant ancestors only 300,000 years ago. Yet, in that time, we established ourselves as the dominant species on this third rock from the sun. You may ask, how is any of this relevant to the subject at hand?

The average human has just seventy-nine short years to write his or her story. Seventy-nine years is just a blink of an eye to the universe. And time is always ticking away from us as we navigate the complexities of life. Sometimes, the story is cut short, either by our own hands or those of another. Sometimes, the story lasts long after the thrill of living has gone. And sometimes, we are given a chance to make an indelible mark on history.

More often than not, however, we fail to seize the opportunities, or the time, afforded us by the universe. Timid by nature, we gravitate toward the people who look, talk, and think like us. We eschew the difference and retreat to the safety of our herd mentality.

And in doing so, we forfeit the adventure that life should be.

The empirical evidence establishes that time is not our friend, yet we continue to allow the concept of time to rule our lives. We convince ourselves that time is infinite and that we have no expiration date to use it. We convince ourselves that *tomorrow* there will be plenty of time to accomplish what we want and live the life we deserve.

Tomorrow. The answer is always *Tomorrow*.

This, of course, is a lie that hides our insecurities and imperfections behind a veil of denial. The inconvenient truth is that we are fragile beings, and a lifetime of hopes and dreams can be lost in the blink of an eye.

I, too, am guilty of this delusion. I've spent most of my days pursuing some distraction to escape the harsh realities of this world. I cannot tell you how many days I sat looking at these four walls, drinking whiskey and hoping that the monsters outside would disappear. But between you and me, the monsters never really go away. Oh, they may fade into the background as you struggle to remember your name in an alcohol-induced stupor, but they are always watching you. The monsters always await you to summon up the courage and venture outside.

Someone once asked me, *'If you could do it all over again, would you change anything?'*

My response surprised me: "There are no do-overs in life, but there are second chances. I cannot change what I have done, but I can only hope to do better with this second chance that I have been given.

"My regret is not in pulling the trigger that night. I regret waiting for so much of my life to pass before taking that stand. I have never been whom I wanted to be, and I have never wanted to be who I am. But I am trying, and that should count for something in this world."

What Does Anything Mean?

What does anything mean? A better question is, why should it mean anything? Life is precious, a gift to be cherished. Unfortunately, we take it for granted; we waste it on trivial matters from day to day. We forget to say or do the things that we should because, as I've established, there is a belief that tomorrow will always come; until it doesn't.

As of this writing, it's been five years since I shot my way from obscurity to fame. All I had to do was kill four people to get there, and I have carried the weight of that decision with me every day since I woke up in the hospital. Don't get me wrong now, knowing what would happen next; I could still pull that trigger today. It doesn't mean that I am comfortable with what I have done; it just means that I have accepted what I have done. How many of you can say the same thing?

To that end, I have some news to share. I finally married on April 29th of last year. It was a small ceremony. Twenty of our closest friends and family attended as we tied the proverbial knot at a small bed and breakfast in upstate New York. Ah, but who was the bride?

About a year ago, I learned that many people had taken an active interest in my love life. I was having lunch with Traci when our waitress leaned over and whispered in my ear, "I'm Team RaD."

She then proceeded to give Traci the side-eye as she refilled my tea. As the waitress walked away, Traci looked at me and asked, "What the Hell was that about?"

Confused, I said, "I have no fucking idea."

Taking a drink of water, Traci asked, "What did she say to you?"

"She said something about being team RaD?"

Traci laughed so hard that she spit out the water across the table. I asked, "What's so funny?"

Traci went on to explain that much like with the books and movies of *Twilight*, people had become emotionally invested in who I should be dating. According to Traci, there were four distinct "teams," each with a different preferred romantic partner for me. The teams were known as TaD, RaD, MaD, and BaD.

I laughed, "You're fucking with me, right?"

Still wiping water off the table with her napkin, Traci said, "No. It's really a thing."

Perplexed, I asked, "So what do all these *'ads'* mean?"

"Well, the two most popular groups, or teams as they prefer to be called, are TaD and RaD. TaD is an acronym for Traci and David; RaD is for Robyn and David. The waitress told you she wants you to be with Robyn, not me."

"What the fuck?" I scoffed. "People actually waste their time on my love life?"

Traci had finally managed to take a drink without spitting it all over the table.

"Yes, they do."

Still trying to peel back the layers of this onion, I asked, "How do you know about this, and I don't?"

Right about this time, the waitress returned with our check. She smiled at me and then tossed the bill in Traci's direction. Traci retrieved the statement, and under her breath, she said, "Nice."

Now utterly aware of what was happening, I asked. "What's up?"

Traci handed me the bill, "See for yourself."

Looking at the bill, I could see that the waitress had comped my meal, and, at the very bottom of the invoice, she had written in big, bold letters: *TEAM RAD, BITCH!*

I laughed, and Traci threw her napkin at me. "It's not that funny," she said.

"Yes. Yes, it is."

Traci giggled and then gave me this mischievous look.

"What?"

Traci replied, "I'm so going to kiss you in front of that bitch!"

"And I'm so okay with that. But first, you've got to tell me, what do MaD and BaD mean?"

Traci continued, "Well, I don't know how to put this, but…there is a certain group of people who think you should be dating Alice. MaD stands for Miller and David."

"Alice? Alice Miller? Why her?"

"During the trial," Traci explained. You and Alice passed notes back and forth. Well, some people thought those were love notes."

"It was trial, not fucking high school!"

Traci reassured me, "I know. I know. But some people only see and hear what they want, and that was enough for some to believe that you and Alice were secretly dating then and continue to do so today."

"Okay, let's just work off that premise for a moment," I said, head shaking. "How do these people explain, you?"

"Well, it would be inappropriate for an Attorney, Alice, to have an affair with her client, you. So, the prevailing theory is that you and Alice got me to be the focal point of your love life to continue your illicit affair without public scrutiny. According to this belief, I am just a diversion to protect your true love interest."

I laughed, "That's ludicrous."

Traci snickered, "Oh, that's nothing compared to what Team BaD wants to see happen."

I sighed, "What?"

"Remember when we had dinner with Brad Caspar?"

So, a little context is necessary for the rest of this conversation to make any sense. As I said in my last book, a movie deal was in the works. That concept finally got the green light, and, as of this writing, filming had wrapped a couple of months ago. Early on in the project, Brad Caspar had been asked to play the role of a certain Assistant District Attorney. As you know, Brad Caspar bears a striking resemblance to Brad Pitt, but with one major difference: one was once married to Jennifer Aniston, and the other was not.

Brad, (Caspar, not Pitt), the Executive Producer, the Director, Traci, and, of course, I went to dinner to discuss the role. At some point during the evening, Brad got up from the table to answer the call of mother nature. As he did, he kind of stumbled a little bit and put his hand on my shoulder to steady himself. The Paparazzi got a picture of this interaction, and the tabloids then ran wild with speculation of Brad Caspar and his "secret" lover, me.

I know this is how tabloids sell magazines, but some people actually believed the article. I got phone calls and emails from complete strangers encouraging me to be brave and to make my sexuality public. Personally, I have never cared much about what people do, whom they love, or how they show their affection. But the thing is, I'm not gay. I like women; I always have.

My friends, of course, had a field day with this irresponsible reporting. Even Traci got into the act, asking me when I was moving in with Brad. It was one big joke that eventually turned into an urban myth. My part in this story eventually faded away, but some people, apparently, have long memories and little else to do but spread lies and innuendo.

This is not who we are, yet this is who we have become. Blame social media if you like. Blame the twenty-four-hour news cycle if you so choose. Blame parents, society, education, incarceration. Blame whomever you like. But the sad truth is this: we are responsible for this debacle. And we, too, are responsible for fixing this mess. Are you up to that challenge? I know, I know, you'll get back to me when the cat video is over.

Anyways, back to our conversation already in progress…

I shook my head, "Are you telling me…?"

Traci began to explain, "There is a small, but vocal group of people who think that you and Brad Caspar are romantically involved because of that photograph and article. BaD actually stands for."

I put my elbows on the table, cradled my head in my hands, and started mumbling, "Brad and David?! No, no, no, no, this can't be happening."

Amused, Traci interrupted, "It's okay, I understand. I'd leave you for Brad too…"

I looked up, clasped my hands just below my chin, and said, "You are having too much fun with this."

Traci laughed, reached across the table, placed her right hand on my left cheek, and whispered, "I love you. But I couldn't resist."

"How do you know about all of this?"

Traci radiated with satisfaction at my discomfort, "I get more emails and calls about you and our relationship than I get about the stories that I report on. I get a lot from Team TaD encouraging me to marry you as, and I quote: *'your one true love.'* I also get a lot from Team RaD encouraging me to step aside so that you can be with Robyn, who apparently is your one true love—"

"Please stop that—"

"Oh, and I also get emails from Team MaD, asking me to stop pretending and step aside so that you can be with Alice, *your one true love—!*"

"Oh, God," I muttered,

Ignoring my protests, Traci continued.

"But my absolute favorite emails and calls come from Team BaD, asking me to step aside so that you can be with Brad Caspar, *your true love.*"

Rubbing the top of my head with my left hand, I let out a deep sigh, "Anything else you want to tell me about this nonsense?"

Traci smiled, "No matter which team contacts me about you, they always ask the same question."

My head was again cradled by my hands, "What do they ask?"

Beaming joyfully, Traci responded, "What kind of lover are you?"

I threw my hands up in dismay, "That's it! We are *done* with this conversation, and I will pretend that this never happened."

Traci let out a lusty laugh, and as we stood up to walk away, she grabbed my arm and said, "Here comes that waitress."

True to her word, Traci passionately kissed me in full view of the now scowling waitress.

Fast forward from that moment until three in the afternoon, April 29th. Now, be honest with me; you must have a favorite one that stands out above the rest. Whom do you picture walking out that French door at the end of this courtyard? Is it Traci or Robyn? Perhaps Alice Miller or even Brad Caspar?

Let me offer you a hint or two. Yes, Alice Miller was in attendance, just not wearing a wedding gown. As I did not craft the guest list, I can neither confirm nor deny whether Brad Caspar was invited. However, I can assure you that Caspar was nowhere to be found roaming the grounds of this particular bed and breakfast on that special day.

So, which would it be, looking at me, so in love with her, and waiting at the end of this courtyard path? Traci? Or Robyn? You do have a preference, don't you? Close your eyes, picture the scene in your mind, and then say the name of who *you* think should be my beautiful bride. Just speak her name aloud for the world to hear; dreams can't come true unless *you* give life to them.

One last hint, which will give the game away. One person was noticeably absent from this courtyard scene. One person was more than a thousand miles away, completely unaware of what was happening that day. Oh, the suspense is killing you, isn't it? Let me end this suspense before you do something rash, like reading ahead. It was Robyn. Yes, Robyn had been intentionally left off the guest list, which would mean…?

Traci Kaneko-Taylor was my only choice, my one true love, and my extraordinary bride on that special day. Absolutely stunning in that wedding dress, I found myself more in love with her, in that very moment, than I ever thought possible.

She smiled as the doors flung open to reveal a bright blue sky overhead. Instinctively, she looked up as she crossed the threshold before locking eyes with me. I patiently waiting for her to walk across a short courtyard to the altar. She wiped a tear away from her left cheek as she began her journey toward her newest adventure, marriage.

Now, if I am completely honest, I have been in love with Traci long before that fateful event, more than four years ago. She was a local celebrity, someone that I had seen often on TV, and she became a fantasy that was always just beyond my reach. I actually met her once at a college football game. She and her boyfriend were sitting one row in front of me, her black thong peeking out just above her jeans for all the world to see.

I found myself just behind her at the concession stand, buying another beer. She turned, looked at me, and said hello. Frozen by fear, all I could muster was, "It's been a good game."

"Yes, it has," she replied.

And then she was gone. I still remember the sight of that black thong over her jeans to this very day. I could not tell you who won the game, the final score, or who played quarterback for either team. I doubt she would ever remember that conversation or me, but I could tell you every detail about her face, hair, clothes, and body on that day.

When the reception ended and we were finally alone, I admitted to this brief encounter. Traci smiled and said, "It's been a good game."

"What did you say?"

I cried a lot as Traci revealed.

"Yes, I remember that day. Yes, I remember you. When I first saw you, I thought you were cute. When I saw you flub your way through our first conversation, I thought you were adorable. And with each passing day, I found myself more and more attracted to you. And as I walked away from you, I remember thinking: '*This is someone I could marry someday.*'"

When a woman of celebrity status puts her emotions above the laws of reality, time, and space, open up to you for just a moment as the tumblers click into place. And, in the blink of an eye, you catch a glimpse of your true purpose within the universe. Yet, when your eyes open again, it's gone.

Where's Robyn?

That is a good question; I certainly do not know the answer. Shortly before my first book was published, I gave Robyn an advanced copy to read. She sent back the following email:

> I know this is coming out of the left field, but...
>
> At this point, I need to cut all ties with you... not at his request, but mine. I cannot do this again. Tom and I have an amazing relationship, and I cannot jeopardize it again. Although I should be able to have other men that are just friends, you and I are in a different situation, you know? I feel that I have been very disrespectful to Tom. He has been MORE than tolerant/friendly about it.
>
> I wish you every happiness and the best in your new adventures, whatever they might be. I sincerely

hope that you and your family work things out. Really, be in good health and happiness.

Again, I know this is coming out of nowhere… there are no good words; to reiterate, Tom did not ask me to do this. I have to. Please don't think badly of me. This probably should have happened a while ago. There was no good time, as I never wanted to hurt your feelings.

My thoughts and prayers are always with you.

Robyn

Not exactly what I was expecting, but perhaps I was being a bit naïve. I had been complicating a marriage I should have left alone years ago. I could not distance myself from my feelings for Robyn. It was wrong of me and undoubtedly selfish, but it felt right then. My response also startled me:

It's hard to believe that I can say this and mean it, but the last thing I want to do is cause problems for you with Tom. I don't know if you reflect on life the same as I do, but my mortality scares me, especially the closer I get to the end. But the inevitable loss of friends, family, and you (I have created a whole new category just for you) terrifies me.

And now it appears as if that inevitable day, metaphorically speaking, has come. There are so many things that I have wanted to say to you over these many years but to find the right words which can match the intent and meaning of what I have to say eludes me. Perhaps, it is because this relationship defies a logical explanation.

Truth be told, I never understood why it was me. What exactly did you see in me that I still can't see in myself today? Sometimes it's best not to question the why, but I know I am better because of you.

Perhaps, it's because the words do not exist. Of the thousands and thousands of terms developed over the centuries, maybe the right words, with the correct meaning, have eluded mankind because mere words were not enough to describe our unique relationship. Although it's a quest I gave up some time ago, my long and futile pursuit of you led to something unexpected: a bond that cannot be broken by time, distance, or any mortal man (woman maybe, but no man).

I have never lied to you about anything, even when it makes me look foolish. So, I see no reason to sugarcoat my feelings now. Over the years, I have loved and hated you, but I have always needed you. I still need you today, but I have proven I can live without you.

Do know this: I am just an email or phone call away if you should ever need me. No matter where I am in this world, if you need me, then I will always be there for you. And, even in your darkest hour, when the universe has turned its back on you, and it seems as if God herself has forsaken you, I will always come if you ask me to.

Or perhaps it's because this is not really the end; it's just a pause. A temporary interruption, if you will, to allow the universe's time to catch its breath so that it does not collapse under the weight of this paradox that we have created. But if this is indeed goodbye, I want to thank you for everything you have done for me over the years.

There are so many things that I would thank you for, but I specifically want to thank you for saving me from the person that I had become. I do not know what

I will amount to in this life, but without you, it would not matter.

And I suppose it was foolish of me to think I ever really stood a chance, but I would also like to thank you for that one perfect kiss on the dance floor and that one perfect night at the beach.

When I look back at my life, those two moments are my proudest accomplishments. To share that deep connection with another human being is all I had ever wanted, and it was worth all the heartache that followed.

The David Bowie *song "Heroes" was inspired by a couple together at the Berlin Wall (ironically enough, a married man and a woman who was not his wife). I thought this fitting of us, our complicated relationship, and the insurmountable wall of reality we must face. So, I would leave you with this:*

Though nothing, nothing will keep us together,
We can beat them forever and ever,
Oh, we can be heroes, just for one day…

May the road rise to meet you, and the wind always be at your back. May the sunshine warm your face, and may the rains fall soft upon your fields. And until we meet again, may God hold you in the palm of Her hand. I will see you again, in this life or the next.

David

And those, my friends, were the last words between Robyn and me. It has been over two years now, and I see no end in this enigma. She has chosen her path, and I have chosen mine. These two paths may meet once again. Until then, I will carry on as best that I can.

Two Worlds Collide

I am fascinated by the enigmas of life. It all seems so random how events unfold before our very eyes. Life can wrap around us in the sun's warmth or smother us in the bitter cold; it can build you up into a mountain or tear your soul down to the ground. It's a mystery how all the gears and cogs interact and how they mesh together to form this reality.

Far more impressive, to me at least, is the unpredictable impact of strangers and how they can affect our lives; even without ever meeting one another, one person can forever alter the trajectory of another. This web of opaque interconnectivity flows through the width and breadth of the universe as events develop and evolve independently of one another.

There is a theory that insists that when a butterfly flaps its wings in a Costa Rican jungle, and it sets in motion a chain of events that leads to a Category 5 hurricane slamming into New York City; or not. It's the uncertainty of it all, how the waves of time and space start a ripple here and finish as a tsunami there, on the other side of the world. Theorists refer to this interaction as the butterfly effect, but I prefer to think of it as the collision of two worlds.

We can idly sit by and wait for two worlds to collide and disappear, much like two icebergs meeting in the dead of night. If no one saw it, then did it really happen? And if it didn't happen, then why do we care? I care because I know firsthand the carnage caused by the collision of two worlds and the chaotic aftershocks of such an event. Even if you didn't see it happen, you have to open your mind to the possibility of such a calamity. The world is much bigger than either you or me, and collisions, large and small, occur every day.

It is here, at this moment of a singular collision, that I found myself more than one thousand miles away…

What Happened?

I was with a friend in a midtown bar, sharing more than a few laughs and nearly as many drinks as we hit the pause button for the afternoon on this thing called Life. I was pointing out the irony of drinking a Manhattan, in Manhattan, mid-day, while in a midtown bar when my phone rang. It was my mother, so I left it to go voicemail. A couple of minutes later, she called again.

My friend asked, "Shouldn't you answer that?"

I looked at the phone, "No, I'll call her back later tonight."

A few minutes later, the phone rang again. This time, it was Traci calling me. Still not interested in hitting the play button on Life, I let it go to voicemail. A few seconds later, I received a text from Traci. Noticeably short and to the point, the text read:

ANSWER YOUR FUCKING PHONE!

Moments passed, and the ringing began again. This time, I answered.

"Hey, what's up?"

"You need to call your mom!" Traci barked. "*Now!*"

The disturbing tone in Traci's voice gave away the urgency of the request. Genuinely concerned, I asked, "Why? What happened?"

Trying to hold back her emotions, Traci stammered, "It's your dad. He's been in a car accident. David, it's bad."

I had now fully engaged that play button for *Life* once again.

"How bad?"

By this point in the conversation, Traci was sobbing.

"Just call your mom, and then please come home."

My hands were trembling as I dialed my mom's number. She picked up on the first ring.

"David, we need to talk."

Her voice was hollow and frail; I could tell she had been crying.

"Mom, what happened?" I whispered. "Is everything okay?"

"Your father…"

I could feel my heart racing, terrified by what I knew was coming next,

"David, your father is…" she stammered.

A shudder burst from my heart and washed over my body like a tidal wave.

I desperately pleaded for an answer, "Mom… *what happened?*"

"David… your father. He's-he's dead."

And there it was, that expected explosion of emotion as the words crashed against the jagged rocks of my soul, *"How? What happened?"*

I really don't know why I kept asking the same question over and over again. I hoped for a different answer each time but always knew how this would end. I remember feeling that same sense of dread and uncertainty, wondering what would happen next when Stacey called me years ago with the news of Jane's death.

For some fucking reason, I distinctly remember looking at my watch; it said 1:47. What happened after that? Well, I'm not entirely sure. I remember a swirl of motion around me; I could hear my mom talking but could not process the words in my mind. I was stuck in an emotional loop between denial and reality, aware of what was happening yet incapable of rejoining the world under these circumstances.

I woke up the next morning in my bed, my childhood bed. Traci was there, sleeping next to me. God, even asleep, she looks so beautiful. I sat up, rubbed my eyes, and tried to remember how I ended up more than one thousand miles from my last clear memory.

I had only a vague recollection of packing, a hazy memory of boarding a plane, and a distant vision of hugging my mom upon arrival. I do not remember unpacking or going to bed. Yet here I am in Florida. How, exactly, did that happen?

"Hey," Traci whispered, "go back to sleep."

"I can't."

Traci said, "Yes. Yes, you can."

I responded, "Not now, maybe tomorrow. Or the next day."

Traci sat up and kissed me on the cheek, "I love you."

I kissed Traci on the forehead, "I love you too. Go back to sleep."

Traci laid back down, closed her eyes, and went back to sleep. I got up and headed for the kitchen. The smell of fresh coffee wafted through the house; the aroma triggered a childhood memory of mornings in the Taylor house. As expected, I found my mom pouring a cup of coffee into the kitchen. "Please pour me a cup."

"Sure, still lots of cream and sugar?"

"Yes, please," I responded, wiping the sleep from my eyes.

My Mom asked, "Do you want to talk about what happened?"

I had so many questions, but I grabbed the cup and said, "No."

"Can I?"

"Of course," I said.

She began, "It's hard to think about it. I will never see your father again. Lord knows he was no saint, but I loved him nonetheless."

"I know."

She continued, "We were together for so long, I just don't know how I will adapt to his absence."

"It sounds cliché, but you will."

My mom coughed, "I know. But it will take time."

"Are you okay? You've been coughing a lot lately."

She responded, "Yeah, I'm fine. Just allergies, you know?"

I'm no Doctor, but that cough sounded a lot worse than just allergies to me. I started to say something about it, I wanted to say something about it, but I couldn't get the words to come out. Instead, I went with, "Mom, what happened with Dad? I mean, how did this happen?"

"I already told you this, David."

I replied, "I know you did, Mom. It's just… I don't really remember the details of our conversation."

She took a sip of coffee, "What do you mean you don't remember?"

Embarrassed, I let out a sigh, "I… I kind of… lost my connection to reality in that moment."

She put the coffee cup on the counter, "What do you mean?"

Trying to explain my mental block, I continued, "After you told me about… Dad, I kind of shut down… mentally and emotionally."

Clearly concerned about my well-being, she asked, "Are you okay?"

Frustrated by my inability to explain myself adequately, I said, "I'm fine now. It's just that… at the time, I didn't really comprehend the details. I understood what happened but was so lost in my thoughts that I failed to connect with the world around me.

"I don't know how I came to be here today. I remember, well, I remember, but it feels more like a distant dream than reality. Does any of this make sense to you?"

She smiled, placed her hand on my cheek, and said, "More than you will ever know."

I closed my eyes and let the warmth of her hand wash over the jagged rocks of my soul. I placed my hand over hers and said, "I love you, Mom."

"I love you too, son."

The Funeral

My father was laid to rest on a Friday; the crystal blue sky overhead was flooded with a brilliant yellow sun that illuminated this ceremony of death. In this sacred place, my father would forever slumber beside his parents and his beloved brother, David Alan Taylor. Yes, I was named after the uncle whom I could never know. Unfortunately, my Uncle David had moved beyond this mortal coil a year before I was born.

I had always felt a certain reverence in any cemetery; there was an undeniable peace within my heart as I walked among the marble and granite markers, tributes to the lives lost over time. We all end up here, in this place, yet none of us know how long or exactly when the journey ends. And that is the mystery of life and death. How much time do you really have? And who, ultimately, decides?

It was a beautiful ceremony, one drenched in pomp and circumstance, and my dad would have hated every minute of it. My father was a lot of things, but a firm believer in formality and decorum was not how he lived his life. However, all the fishing, the womanizing, the drinking, the gambling, and the business, always the business, were his reasons for living. He was a maverick, a liar, a cheater, a conscious objector, and a malcontent of the highest order. Yet, he was my father, and I loved him. Better still, I was his son, and he loved me. Imperfect as this relationship was, who could ask for anything more?

Traci held my hand tight, and Stacey hugged me as I looked over my father's grave. In the distance, I could hear birds singing, and as I looked up, I watched as they took flight into the clear blue sky. Blue was always my favorite color, but, just for today, I would ask to see any other color that did not match my mood. Yet, it seems the world has its own ideas about what you should or shouldn't see.

Fucked up world we live in, isn't it?

A Musical Interlude

"Ticking away the moments that make up a dull day
Fritter and waste the hours in an offhand way.
Kicking around on a piece of ground in your hometown
Waiting for someone or something to show you the way...."

When I am in such a mind as of that day, my thoughts retreat to this song and its connection to my father. It would be years before I could really appreciate the nuances and complexities of the lyrics, but this song was embedded in my mind from an early age.

A man capable of such emotional highs and lows, my father felt a certain sadness represented by this song. A sadness that I could not truly understand until after his death. My father was a man who was so successful at business, yet, by all accounts, a failure in his personal life. A failure for me, as a son, and a failure for my mother, as a husband.

Yet, once one passes beyond the veil, we tend to overlook the faults of the fallen. We lionize the dead and celebrate their lives in a manner that forgives their shortcomings in this world. We can excuse their behavior and forgive their deeds, but we cannot truly forget the sins committed by the dead. We can try, but we rarely achieve that level of enlightenment.

The Box

The next day, we began the process of removing my father from this world. We went through his clothes, papers, and his life's remnants. Most of it was what an ordinary person would consider junk: awards, newspaper articles, and the like. But some of them had an emotional connection to the family. Things like cameras, photos, jewelry, and money were hidden away in the strangest of places. It was just like a macabre Easter egg hunt, looking for trinkets in closets and cabinets, never sure if you would find the occasional treasure or the rotten egg.

Once I figured out my dad's password, I was able to access his computer. Not sure what I would find, I began to explore the digital wasteland, looking for answers to the many questions that troubled my mind. And here, on his computer, I would find far more answers than I ever expected.

I knew my dad had fancied himself a photographer, and I found thousands of pictures to support his belief. He took pictures of everything: brick walls, trains, beaches, roads, and people. Lots and lots of people, all completely unaware that he had captured a brief moment in time from their ordinary day. A child eating an ice cream cone, an old man reading a book in the park, a young woman sitting outside a café sipping wine. He took great care to capture these subjects, as he documented their ordinary lives, unscripted and authentic. Clearly, this was more than just a hobby for him; it was a passion that, for whatever reason, he chose not to share with others.

I clicked on a folder labeled "Jabber & Twaddle," and what I found genuinely shocked me. Apparently, my dad had another secret locked away and hidden from the world. No, not porn (you sick bastards). Why does everything with you always end up in porn? To my surprise, it seems my dad was a prolific writer.

There was an abundance of random thoughts, fragments of stories, and observations of everyday life, written in a manner guaranteed to offend almost everyone in some form or fashion. So, I should apologize for the offensive words of my father that you are about to read. Yes, I should apologize; but I won't.

You deserve the ugly truth of it all, not the sanitized version people peddle today. Yes, life is not fair; the best you can hope for is to die in your sleep. But while you are alive, you are either a wolf or a sheep. You are either the hunter or the hunted. My Dad, armed with just a keyboard and computer, fancied himself a literary wolf. So, which are you?

I remember my dad talking to me about this dream he had, the darkness of it engulfing everything good and kind in this world. I remember that it really troubled him, the things that he saw in his mind that night, but I never bothered to ask why. When I read this, I finally understood why it weighed so heavily upon his mind:

*

I'm standing on the roof of a stone building; I can smell the ocean almost as much as I can hear the waves crashing on the white sand. I sling my AK-47 over my back, fish out a pack of smokes, and light one up. A shadow moving over the ground catches my attention, and so I look skyward to see six pelicans soaring in formation overhead. The air is cool and crisp this morning, but the sun is shining, and it's beautiful.

Across the way from me is the exact stone building with another lone figure standing in the same position as me. The lookout waves, and as I exhale, I return the friendly gesture. To the left of me are the gardens and, eventually, the beach. To the right is the main building, an imposing stone structure with a stage jutting out from the center. Assembled on the stage is a hulking wooden structure with a man in black perched high atop the raised platform. Positioned back and to the left of the stage stands a drum corps dressed in brilliant red jackets and shiny black hats, waiting patiently for the signal to begin the ceremony.

Gathering in the courtyard below is a festive, boisterous crowd anxiously awaiting the start of this monthly spectacle. And all along the sides of the courtyard are vendors hawking their wares to the eager masses. The air crackles with energy, and the crowd comes to life as the drums beat, calling the faithful to the stage. The drums suddenly stop, and from the right, a tall, thin man clad in a black suit & white shirt walks up to the microphone.

The crowd roars with approval as the man unfurls a piece of parchment and begins to address those in attendance and beyond. As the man speaks, a frail young boy is led to center stage. Crushing out another cigarette, I uttered (almost as if I was afraid that someone might hear), "Christ, I hate it when they bring out the children."

Hero of the Yesterday?

I've seen so many of these that I don't
really bother to listen anymore, but ever
vigilant to do my job, I scan the revelers for
any sign of malcontents. Even over the sound
of my thoughts, I hear bits and pieces. This
frail boy is here for cheating on a test, no
less. Poor bastard, a good grade just isn't
worth the punishment. He is led up the stairs
to the waiting man in black, and as the drums
return to a steady beat, a noose is placed
around the boy's slender neck. Wildly scanning
the courtyard, the boy looks for any sign of
salvation, but none will be found here today.
The drums stop, the man in black pulls the
lever, the boy's falling body jerks to a
sudden stop, and the crowd screams with
delight.

Next, they bring out a young girl. Proud
and defiant to the end, she spits in the face
of the man in black as the noose is placed
around her neck. The drums stop, and the man
in black pulls the lever, but she does not die
quickly. From underneath the girl's long,
black dress, her feet kick franticly as she
tries to reach the step that no longer
remains. Only after a few minutes—and one
final kick—did her lifeless body twist in the
wind: the long dress now a black sail of

death. And then, once again, the crowd screams with delight.

Number three would not go quietly; he kicks and screams at his captors, foaming at the mouth like a rabid dog. But alas, his fight would prove useless, as he too would be pulled to the top of the platform and fitted with a noose. The familiar drums stop, the lever is pulled, and the crowd goes wild again.

The day's final judgment would prove controversial even by our well-established standards. This one would be different; he was no social outcast, a misfit, or a malcontent. The son of a prominent Minister and the captain of the high school football team, this boy commanded respect. The crowd, upon recognizing the condemned, began to call for mercy.

I pull back the bolt on my rifle and chamber a round, waiting for the signal to "disperse" the crowd, but no order would come. The boy would climb the steps with quiet dignity and await his fate. As the lever released, a hush fell over the crowd. One could hear the rope cinch in the silence and snap tight. The boy was now dead, the crowd

left in quiet dismay, and I, unlike four
others, would live to see another day.

Disturbing, huh? Well, I sat down with my
good friend and trusted advisor, Jack Daniels,
for a round table discussion. Round after
round, Jack and I tried to make sense of this
dream, but to no avail. We talked about the
establishment, FCC Sensors, the Government,
disgraced athletes, cheating students, women's
rights in the Middle East, and a host of other
ideas. Still, we simply could not agree on the
symbolism or veiled message hidden within the
content of this dream.

The next day I woke up hungover and still
just as disturbed as I had been the night
before. Crawling out of bed, I muttered, "Fuck
it! I should just lay off the damn chili-
cheese fries before bedtime."

When I was thirteen, I watched Tiger Woods win his first *Masters*
by twelve strokes. I was so excited by Tiger's victory that it
sparked an interest in the sport of golf that resides in me still today.
I had visions of me being the next Tiger Woods, hitting the ball
three hundred fifty yards down the middle of the fairway and

making hundred-foot eagle putts. It was, of course, just a fantasy, but my Uncle Alex humored me by giving me a set of his old clubs. When I say Uncle Alex, he's not my uncle by blood, but he is, or was, like a brother to my dad.

I cried when I read this because I vividly remember that day; I remember Rick and Mary offering me advice on my swing, and I remember my dad trying to keep his composure (and failing miserably) as his swing fell apart over nine holes of golf.

*

"We need to talk."

It's just four simple words, but the combination rates a 9.9 on my anxiety scale when they are put together. I've heard those same four words from a boss just before he fired me. I heard those same four words from a girlfriend just before she broke up with me, and now I've just heard those same four words from my doctor.

I think aloud: "Okay, is this the part where the nice man in a white lab coat tells me I have six months to live?"

"No, it's nothing like that," the good doctor says, "It's just that your blood pressure is a little higher than it should be.

Hero of the Yesterday?

You need to reduce your sodium intake, reduce your drinking, exercise more, and just try to relax."

I replied, "Why don't you just kill me now? I mean, don't you know that everything tastes better with salt on it? Don't you know that a good stiff drink at the end of a busy day is worth its weight in gold? Exercise? Where's the fun in that? And how can I possibly relax? It's a crazy world, full of idiots and sickos just trying to steal what's left of my sanity."

And then the good doctor said, "You see, that's what I'm talking about. Stop watching the news; it's depressing. Why don't you take up a hobby?"

I asked, "Like what? Watching sitcoms?"

"No. Go out and get some exercise. Enjoy yourself. I thought maybe golf would be good for you."

Now, this is something I can get behind, so I go home and tell my wife the Doctor said that I "needed" to play more golf. Okay, my wife's no idiot, but she agrees with the Doctor that I need to do something, and as luck would have it, just a few days prior, my son decided he wanted to be the next Tiger Woods.

He soon gets a set of hand-me-down clubs from my friend Alex and starts begging me to take him to the golf course. I told him that we should start at the driving range, you know, to get a little practice first; I mean, I haven't swung a golf club in anger for nearly two years. My son, being the impatient type, can't wait for the driving range outing and pushes immediately for a day on the golf course. Eventually, my desire to hit the links surpasses my desire to not look like an idiot, and I agree to a weekend safari.

Just down the street, there is a quaint little 9-hole course that the city owns. My son and I show up on a sunny Saturday morning, eager to beat the shit out of a few golf balls. He's hoping it will just be the two of us, but I know we are gonna get stuck with someone. Right on cue, the starter pairs us up with two other misfits: a very nice black guy and a grandmother. I know, I know, it sounds like the beginning of a joke…

A 13-year-old, his father, a black guy, and a grandmother are on a golf course when… (insert punch line here)

On the first tee, one drive sent a woman walking her dog on the other side of the street ducking for cover, and another tee shot nearly killed a squirrel (that was just me). My son eventually put one about 100 feet into the air that landed harmlessly 20 yards in front of us. Rick, the nice black guy, hit a tree on the left. Grandma put one straight down the middle.

The next few holes found most of us playing military golf (you know, LEFT side of the fairway, RIGHT side of the fairway; LEFT bunker, followed quickly by the RIGHT bunker) while Grandma again stroked golf balls down the middle. By the end of the round, I found out that your golf swing goes to hell after a 2-year hiatus, my son heard words that he normally doesn't hear from me, and we both discovered that golf is nothing, but a good walk spoiled (thank you, Mark Twain).

What were the final scores? Well, I beat my son by only two strokes, Rick beat me by at least ten, and Grandma, well, she beat us all. Talk about a humbling experience. Despite my rusty golf swing, my son's rapid improvement, and losing to Grandma, I still had fun.

So, thank you, Doctor. Maybe next time, you can say I need to go to a strip club, smoke a cigar, and drink like a fish. If you say it, then the wife will at least consider it.

Yet, my father did have a serious side to him. Yes, he had a certain irreverence for almost everything in life; the noticeable exception being military service. My father never served in the military, but Uncle Alex did, and my grandfather fought in the jungles of Vietnam. I remember when Grandpa would get drunk, he would tell me stories about Vietnam, stories about places like Khe Sanh and Da Nang. I couldn't sleep for a week after hearing about the people he killed, the friends he lost, and the emotional brutality of war.

The next piece that I wanted to share with you, the reader, was written by my father on Monday, May 29th, 2006. It was perhaps two years after this was written. I remember Alex telling me the story of that day in 2005, showing me the bracelet that he wore and the tears that he cried when he said the names of SFC D. Adams, CPT S. Davidson, SPC W. Earl, and SPC S. McGrath:

> *I was celebrating Memorial Day, the traditional American way: at the beach with the family. However, one member of my extended family was noticeably absent, Alex. Although not family in the traditional sense, Alex is like a brother to me. Alex is a career soldier in the Army, and during the last 12 years, he has been stationed at various Forts throughout the U.S. and has even been deployed to Korea (twice). He has also spent a year in Iraq,*

specifically in Ramadi, located at the very heart of the "Sunni Triangle of Death." During his time in Iraq, Alex survived an IED attack, participated in countless patrols, and upon his return to the States, was awarded the Bronze Star for his service in a combat zone. I am very proud of Alex and his service to this Country, but Memorial Day is not about honoring the survivors of war but the ones that made the ultimate sacrifice.

In a combat zone, soldiers are not afforded the luxury of debating U.S. foreign policy or how best to deal with terrorists. There is no room for the lofty ideals of diplomats nor the blind ambitions of politicians. There is no time to debate ideological differences or the justifications for war. In a combat zone, a soldier doesn't care how history will judge this war; a soldier has time to think about only two things: life and death. Though it is not fair, there is only the stark reality of war. Some of the best people do not come back.

On March 04, 2005, four members of Alex's unit were killed by an IED while on patrol in Ramadi. Alex, who was on the same patrol, did not see the attack; but heard and felt it. He knew from the power of the explosion that someone had died, but it wasn't until later that he would learn the particulars. Killed in action were SFC D. Adams, CPT S. Davidson, SPC W. Earl, and SPC S. McGrath. These men represented the best of what America has to offer, and they should not be relegated to mere statistics. To honor their memory, Alex's unit commissioned the creation of a bracelet that was dedicated to these fine young men. To this day, Alex wears his bracelet, not as a sign of mourning but as a celebration of their lives. To some, it may only be a simple reminder of what was lost that day, but to Alex, it is a complex token of the brotherhood forged by the horrors of combat.

War is never the only option, but sometimes it is the best option. Whether or not this is the case in Iraq is irrelevant. To discuss the validity of this war at this time would dishonor the memory of these men. At least we have the luxury to openly disagree with the powers that be; at least we can scream our disapproval at the top of our lungs for the whole world to hear. And why do we have these freedoms? It's because so many fine young men (and women) have given their lives in defending our rights, our ideals, and our Nation. So, on behalf of a grateful Nation, I say thank you for your sacrifice; your life and death will never be forgotten.

Hero of the Yesterday?

I included this last one because, at the time, it seemed so out of character for my father, but in retrospect, it made perfect sense. To the best of my knowledge, at that moment in this story, my father had never been to Mount Rushmore. I, of course, now know better; this was my father keeping a promise that he had made to himself so many years ago.

*

This is some thirty-two years after the fact, but I was pushed to take a stroll down memory lane today, and it pulled me back to that moment standing below those four faces in stone, basking in that brilliant blue South Dakota sky. I lost something today, someone who will never be replaced, and now I find myself questioning my choices in life. There are so many things that I have done over the years, but so many other things that I wish I had done instead. Knowing what I know now, I'd like to go back to that place and start over again.

Many people played a role, both large and small, in the foundation of this country. For example, Crispus Attucks was recognized as the first American killed in the Boston Massacre. Another Bostonian, Dr. Joseph Warren, surrendered his life for the cause of liberty at the battle commonly referred to as Bunker Hill. Thomas Paine eloquently put to words the feelings of so many people before the Declaration of Independence.

But, of all the people who played a part in our country's founding, none was more important or more famous than George Washington. In those early days of the war, George Washington carried the torch of liberty into the dark night. And when the war was over, George Washington continued his service to this country as the first President of The United States.

To the right of Mr. Washington was the esteemed Thomas Jefferson. The third President, and principal writer of the Declaration of Independence, Thomas Jefferson, was responsible for the westward expansion of the country with the Louisiana Purchase in 1803. A prolific writer, a philosopher, a master of many disciplines, and a great lover of wine, Thomas Jefferson was, by far, my favorite President.

Next in line was Theodore Roosevelt. The twenty-sixth President of The United States, T.R. as he was commonly called, was responsible for the conservation of the natural beauty and resources that abounded in this land. During his tenure as President, T.R. facilitated the creation of eighteen national parks, one hundred fifty natural forests, fifty-one bird preserves, and four game preserves.

And across from Washington was Abraham Lincoln, the savior of our country. The sixteenth President, Abraham Lincoln, fought to preserve the union that Washington had built. Born in a log cabin in Kentucky, Mr. Lincoln would announce the Emancipation Proclamation, ensure passage of the Thirteenth Amendment, and deliver the greatest two hundred seventy-one-word speech ever written by man, the Gettysburg Address. And for all of his greatness, he was shot on a Friday night and then died on a Saturday morning.

To a complete stranger, someone unfamiliar with how certain events in my life fell into place, this might read like just another history lesson; but I assure you it is not. No, a history lesson on any one of these men would take hours, and hundreds of pages, to just scratch the surface of their incredible lives. Instead, I have chosen specific accomplishments in their lives, moments that reflect who I had wanted to be. A leader standing resolute in the face of danger, a writer with grand ideals actually put into words, a fighter looking to preserve the natural beauty of this world, a statesman fighting to keep it all together as the world falls apart at the seams.

To some extent, I accomplished these things, yet I fell well short of the mark that I had set for myself standing below Mt. Rushmore. I suppose, with the cards that I had been dealt by life, that was to be expected. Looking back to that day, to that moment in my life, it would be impossible to understand the choices that I had made in the time without a little perspective. I lived, I tried, and I failed, but I never stopped thinking about that day. I never stopped wondering what my life would have been if I had just stayed on the course and never returned to that house on the beach. Life gets so complicated so quickly, and we don't take the time to savor those special moments as they happen.

Life was simpler back then, and no one expected anything of me (not entirely true, there were two people who expected the world of me), but I was young and in love under that blue South Dakota sky. Funny how time marches on, despite your best efforts to keep it at bay. I hate time; what it does to your mind and to your body. But the cruelest part of this process is what time does to those

memories, how it breaks your heart like a
butterfly on a wheel.

It took some time for me to process the things that I had just read. In retrospect, I should have guessed this sooner, knowing how much interest he showed in my own book-writing process. As I worked on my rough draft, my dad always wanted to read the words that I had written. At first, it was a bit uncomfortable for me to share my words with anyone.

I spent hours and hours reading through the written word that comprised the bulk of this treasure trove. File after file, there was a familiar edginess and wit to the words that appeared on the screen before me. A certain irreverence, definite sarcasm, and a wicked sense of humor that just felt right to me.

Every so often, Traci would come into the office and ask me if I was coming to bed. I assured her I would be there soon, only to have her show up again a couple of hours later, asking the same question. I eventually fell asleep at the desk, only to be roused back to life by the smell of coffee wafting through the air.

I wandered into the kitchen, drawn in by the irresistible aroma of the second-greatest of all inventions. My Mom was waiting, ready with a cup of coffee in hand. She passed me the drink and asked, "So, did you find your dad's writings?"

"You knew?"

She responded, "Of course I did."

"Why didn't you tell me?"

"It wasn't my place to share that information with you."

"Why not?" I pushed.

"Your Dad wanted *you* to discover it."

"Why?"

Mom said, "He thought it would be more meaningful if you found his words without help."

"Sometimes I hate you."

She smiled, "But you love me too?"

I nodded in approval.

She stated, "There is something that you need to read."

Mom led me out to the garage and pointed to the top shelf. It was there, in a shoe box high above the rest, that I found my mission. Inside the box was a 35 mm camera, some undeveloped rolls of film, a journal with *I hope this helps* written on it, and a picture of my dad with… Merle Haggard?

Among the other artifacts in the box was a picture of a girl whose smile was perfectly beautiful. The picture was an extreme close-up of this girl's face, her left hand holding back her hair and her exquisite smile emanating from the picture. On the back of this picture, it said,

Michael, don't fuck this up.

—Merle Haggard.

There were several pictures of this girl and my dad. I found maps, a ticket stub from a Chicago Cubs game, A Flock of Seagulls concert in Nashville, and an autographed Merle Haggard ticket stub from Las Vegas. I found a poker chip from Caesar's Palace and brochures from the Grand Canyon, Yellowstone, and Mount Rushmore. I found a tooth, various matchbooks, and a manuscript. The pages were yellowed by time yet surprisingly well preserved.

"What's this?"

She replied, "It's your father's story."

Curious, I began flipping through the pages.

"Have you read this?"

"No," she said.

I looked at her, "Why not?"

"Because it's your father's story. Not mine."

Both nervous and excited, I asked, "When did he write this?"

She responded, "He started it about six months before you were born and finished just after he met you."

Shocked, I questioned, "After he met me? Wasn't he there when I was born?"

She paused for a moment and then uttered, "No."

Confused, I demanded, "Mom, what aren't you telling me?"

She smiled.

"The answers you seek were typed by your father on those pages in your hand a long time ago. Now, go and read the story of a young heart."

I returned to the house, grabbed my cup of coffee, and headed for my dad's office. I sat down in his chair and looked at the title page. I thought: *Son of a bitch, she wasn't lying.*

There, in the middle of the page, it read: "*The Story of a Young Heart,*" and below it stated: "*Written by Michael Taylor.*"

I took a sip of coffee and turned the page as the story began…

The Story of a Young Heart

Written by Michael Taylor
© 1983

Man does not control his own fate. The women in his life do that for him.

--**Groucho Marx**

Prologue

It was as if God, Herself, had felt the loss of David. Yet, it was just another Tuesday for the rest of the world. Just another weekday interrupted by a cold rain that fell from the slate grey clouds above. Just another day of ants marching from Point A to Point B and then back again without any thought of the symbolism revealed by the rain or the significance of the day. The masses will forever forget the power of this moment in time as they go about their fruitless lives in a hopeless world. And when it was over, if you were to ask them about the day's events, all they would say is, "Didn't it rain today?"

But I remember everything about that day. I remember the sound of the wipers scraping across the windshield, desperately trying to hold back the tears from Heaven. I remember hearing *"Yesterday"* playing faintly in the background as we went to the cemetery. I remember the chill of the rain as I stepped out of the car. I remember the distinct sound of those viscous raindrops as they exploded on the well-kept grass. I remember the solemn parade of markers leading to the grave site. I remember the mournful song of a lonely black bird perched high in a tree. I remember the words spoken by the Priest, how this was God's will and all that bullshit. David was gone, and I could not see any greater good to come of his passing. The world was a colder, darker place now that his story had ended.

Oh, what stories could I tell of our seasons in the sun, of our life in this sleepy, little coastal town? Tales of an ordinary world, in a simpler time of lighted streets on quiet nights. But life is just not that simple, and, alas, the taste is not so sweet. So no, this is not the story of the ants marching in unison or a tale of political intrigue. This is not a story about God's will, a true believer's crisis of faith, or the redemption of another lost soul. This is the story of us; you, me, everyone. This is the story of love, regret, and the call of the great unknown. This is the story of a young heart.

A House is Seldom a Home

Home, home again. I like to be here when I can. The lyrics echoed through my heart as I lay there on my bed. Downstairs, scores of people offered their condolences, with casseroles in hand, and reminisced about their most incredible memories of David. The spectacle was too sickening, so I had retreated to this, my only sanctuary in this house. This was a fine house, to be sure. It was built of concrete, steel, and glass with extraordinary care by master craftsmen. It was built to showcase its striking view of the ocean beyond the dunes by becoming a home for a specific family, my family.

A home is a special place, filthy with a deep emotional connection painted by years of experiences that can only be seen in the mind and felt in the heart. A hundred houses were almost like it on this stretch of beach, and thousands more just beyond the horizon, but so few could genuinely be called a home. Six weeks ago, I proudly called this place my home. Today, it was now just four walls and a roof, simply a place where I retreated to protect myself from the harsh realities of the outside world. This house could never again feel like home to me.

My home would now be the earth beneath my feet, whether under the brilliant sun or a moonlit sky. My home was one hundred ninety-seven million square miles on this third rock from the sun, just waiting for me to explore. And if the land were my home, then the sea would be my church, for it is in the ocean where I would go to pray and feel the power of God as the cleansing waves would rush over my soul.

And it was in the sea, in this moment of sorrow, that I wanted to speak to God. I tried to tell Her that She was wrong and had no right to take David away: my older brother, my *only* brother. And yet, for reasons unknown, She felt it necessary to break my heart and harden my soul. We have a lot to discuss, the two of us, and I know that you will not like what I have to say.

Knock – Knock – Knock!

The tapping on my bedroom door woke me from my trance-like state.

"Michael?"

I let out a heavy sigh, "Yes, Mom?"

"Michael, people are asking about you."

I replied, "Tell them I'm grieving."

"Michael, they want to talk to you."

I retorted, "I don't want to talk to people. Not today."

"Michael... he was my son."

Finally, I stated, "But you had more than one son. I only had one brother."

I wanted to take back the words as I said them, but some things, no matter how hard you try, cannot be undone. I could hear her crying as she slowly closed the door and walked away. A wicked thought crossed my mind as I stared at the ceiling: *You can be such a fucking asshole when you want to be.*

Resigned to my fate, I got up and then reluctantly headed downstairs.

As I descended the stairs, I could hear a cacophony of voices rising to greet me. That sickening feeling was bubbling up again, but I swallowed hard and forged my way through the crowd to my mom. I hugged her, wiped away the tears I had caused, and whispered in her ear, "I'm sorry. I didn't mean it."

She smiled an uncertain smile, one born of pain and relief. She kissed my cheek and whispered back, "I love you."

I nodded my head as I wiped away the tears from my eyes.

But before I could turn to walk away, I felt a slight tap on the back of my shoulder. "How are you holding up, Mike?"

It was that fucking Priest. Of all the people in this house, why did it have to be that fucking Priest?

"As well as can be expected. My brother drowned, his body was never recovered, and you presided over the burial of an empty casket today. Any other questions? Or were you just being polite?"

There was that wicked thought again; I'm such a fucking asshole sometimes.

The Priest put his hands together as if in prayer, nodded in agreement.

"I understand your pain, Michael," he spoke softly with an edge of pain to his voice. "My brother also died when I was young. Cancer."

Oh, now, don't I feel like a dick? Trying to recover, "I didn't know that. I'm sorry."

"It took many years for me to accept that it was God's will. Some people, like my brother and David, seem too good for this Earth. There can be no other reason why they would die so young, with so much life to live."

A curious look fell over my face as I contemplated his theory, but my cynical mind dismissed it as a random tragedy, not bound to any divine intervention. But still, part of me wanted to believe the fucking Priest. The child deep inside me wanted to believe, but the teenage malcontent I had become would not accept such an excuse.

The rest of the afternoon disappeared in a haze of sympathy. Everyone there was so concerned about consoling me that no one ever thought of what I might need: several good stiff drinks. It was nearly eleven before I found myself sitting alone on the beach with a pilfered bottle of whiskey in one hand and a cola in the other. I looked out over the waves, staring at the moon, and contemplated joining David in a watery grave. In the back of my mind, I heard a strange voice say, *Fuck that!*

I fell back on the beach, closed my eyes, and tried to focus on this new voice in my head. I could hear the fizz of the cola and the gurgle of the bottle as its precious contents leaked out onto the pure white sand. I could feel the breeze blowing my hair across my face and the rumble of the ocean through the sand. I could smell the salt in the air, and somewhere in the distance, I could smell the remnants of a beach bonfire. And that strange voice once again said, "Fuck that!"

Now most sane people would seek immediate help. I, on the other hand, leaned into the chaos unfolding in my mind and asked a simple question, "Fuck what?"

"That idea... that stupid idea floating around in your fucked-up head."

"I'm afraid you will need to be more specific; I have a lot of fucked-up ideas in my head," I snickered as I spoke the words.

"It's not your time; that's not the death you will see."

"It's as good as any," I retorted.

"Oh, you don't get off that easy. There is so much for you to learn, so much more to see, so much more for you to love."

"What if..." I drifted off to sleep, drunk and stupid once again.

I did not wake up until I felt the rising tide rushing against my body. I sat up, shook my head, and looked around, "What the fuck was that?"

I stumbled back to the house, showered, and fell into bed. It would be well past noon before I would open my eyes again.

Keys to the Car

David had one prized possession, a nineteen sixty-six Ford Mustang convertible. It was the only car he had ever wanted to drive, so he scoured the newspaper for months to find the right vehicle. When he was barely fifteen, David talked our dad, technically our mom, into buying his dream car. Candy apple red, with a black interior and top, I loved to hear that v-8 engine growl as he shifted gears and pushed the gas pedal to the floor. I learned to drive in that car; I went to Prom in that car and got laid for the first time in the back seat.

I did say that I went to Prom in that car, right?

The truth is, I love that car almost as much as my brother ever did. Some of my fondest memories of him revolve around that car; now, it was mine. It was still titled to my dad legally, but David had made it known that if anything ever happened to him, the car should go to me.

But I hadn't taken the keys yet, and it felt offensive to me even to think about driving that car while the search for David continued. Even after the search had been called off, I still felt uneasy about sitting behind the wheel. However, now that he had been declared dead and ceremoniously, if not officially, buried, it felt like the right time to honor his memory with a quick lap around "the circuit," as we liked to call it.

What started as my driving lessons, the circuit was an oddly shaped figure eight that weaved from back-road to back-road and then back to town again. At first, it was just a random pattern, but the course took shape over months as we explored the two-lane roads that dotted the inland landscape. The circuit tested the will of the man, not the limitations of the machine, so the challenge, for lack of a better word, was how fast are you willing to go? The success or failure of any lap depended upon eclipsing the hundred-mile-an-hour mark.

Sounds simple enough, right? But it takes a while for the car to get up to that speed, and only a couple of roads within the circuit offer you the time and space needed to reach that mark. One of those roads dipped down and then crested with a sizable hill at that critical moment of success or failure. It felt like driving over a railroad track at a legally posted speed. At one hundred miles an hour, however, it felt like a fighter jet being launched from an aircraft carrier.

As the passenger, you could close your eyes and feel that moment, however briefly, when the wheels left the ground. As the driver, you were terrified, screaming at the top of your lungs, *"Holy fucking shit!"*

The other road offered a different test of your courage. Straight, but shorter with a sharp right turn at the end, the question was, do I dare get up to the speed of success, or do I live with the failure? On this part of the circuit, it was now the driver who felt the rush of the challenge, completely in control of what happened next. The passenger, however, white-knuckled it down the length of the road, jamming on that imaginary brake that we've all used before when we had to surrender our sense of control and subsequently place our life in the hands of another.

It's odd how the same experience could radically differ based on which seat you were in for that lap. And today, for the first time, only one of us would make a lap on the circuit.

It didn't feel right making this trip without David somehow being a part of it. So, I did something I hadn't done since the beginning of this ordeal; I went into David's room. I looked around; the room was exactly as last night when he said goodbye to me. And though I knew Mom had hung his jacket on the back of the door, it felt like David was still there. This house once more felt like a home for a brief second, but the moment passed quickly, and I again felt that soul-crushing sorrow washing over me.

I grabbed his jacket hanging on the door, the one the police found on the beach that morning, then the keys, and headed for the car in the driveway. Once there, I strapped the jacket using the passenger lap belt and began our pre-trip checklist. Top down, check. Radio working; check. Checklist complete. I hesitated momentarily, inserted the key, and then turned the ignition.

The car sprang to life, the engine responding with a growl every time I pressed the gas pedal. I laughed as the memories flooded my mind, and then I cried, knowing that this was all that I had left of David, those memories. I sat there for a few moments, not knowing what to do. I forced myself to put the car into first gear, pulled out of the driveway, and then headed out of town toward the starting point of the circuit.

No lap around the circuit was complete unless the appropriate music was played at the highest possible volume. David and I had worked for hours putting together mixtapes trying to match the speed, the turns, and the pace of the circuit to music. By the twenty-ninth attempt, we had the perfect combination of songs, and in the proper order, to enhance the twists and turns of the road.

I crossed over the causeway bridge and readied to turn left, marking the start of the circuit. As I made the turn, I popped cassette tape # 29 into the tape deck, and as the first song began to play, I hit the gas. The engine growled as I changed gears and sped down the lonely two-lane road racing toward my destiny.

A Gift? For Me?

After successfully violating several motor vehicle laws, I made my way back to the house. I parked the car in its usual spot and sat there momentarily, contemplating the day's events. Yes, things would never be the same, but I had the memories of David to hold on to, the memories which might provide a semblance of normalcy in my otherwise fucked-up life.

For some odd reason, I thought it was fitting for David's jacket to remain in the car. It wasn't very practical to leave it buckled in the front seat, and the jacket was too big for the glove box, so where should I put it? Then I had an idea; I unbuckled the jacket from the safety of the lap belt and moved to put it in the trunk. I opened the trunk and tossed in the jacket. Just as I went to close the trunk, I saw something that didn't belong there. It was a package covered in pink unicorn wrapping paper with the message, "For Michael."

I chuckled; I knew exactly what it was. Well, sort of. From the size, shape, and weight, it was definitely a book of some kind. Probably a copy of, *Are you there, God? It's me, Margaret,* or some other nonsense from David.

When I was thirteen, David started telling me that he really wanted a sister, not a brother. As a joke, he would give me birthday gifts befitting a sister. Things like a make-up kit, a purse, or a bottle of perfume. But my personal favorite, though, was the princess costume, complete with a tiara.

Why did any of this matter? Well, David disappeared two weeks before my birthday. This must have been the latest in a long line of sister-related gifts David had planned to give me. Unfortunately, as fate would have it, he would not have the opportunity to do so in person. Painful as it was to acknowledge, this would be the last gift he would ever give me. I was tempted to open it, to reveal what would be his last joke on me. But, somewhere deep inside, I felt the need to keep the mystery alive, if just for a little longer.

School

I had been in and out of school for the last six weeks.

When the Coast Guard launched their search for David, I sat at home waiting for news. Once they called off their search, my dad hired private pilots to continue looking for David. I went up in those planes, scanning the horizon for any sign of life. And to my dismay, I found none. Eventually, my family had to accept the reality of that awful realization: David was not coming home, and the closure we so desperately needed would not come easily.

During this process, the faculty at school had been very supportive of my family's efforts. They allowed me to continue my studies at home by offering any assistance, educationally, that I might need. The truth was, the school was not hard for me; I could handle any assignment half asleep, which was part of my problem. I was not challenged by the material presented to me; I was bored with the minutia of it all.

But now, with David's death behind us, I was expected to return to class. Everyone, teachers, and students alike, tread carefully around my presence. No one wanted to mention his name directly to me, but everyone talked about his fate.

What happened? Why was nobody found? My feelings on the subject were never really a consideration, yet I was returning to a place that did not matter anymore to me.

There are certain advantages to being the younger sibling of a person so beloved by teachers and students alike.

My brother was an exemplary student that did and said all the right things. He had sought academic excellence in his education, and David had also exhibited a gregarious personality, able to penetrate the hardest of hearts with his wit and charm.

In addition, David was a star athlete in baseball, football, and soccer. He had thrived in that athletic environment fostered by camaraderie and teamwork. I could never understand why, but David had always preferred sports that involved the participation of others.

In this regard, we could not be more opposite. I had always been drawn to activities like golfing, fishing, and surfing, which relied heavily on the individual's talent over that of a collective team. I simply could never trust others with the success or failure of my efforts. I wanted to win or lose, based solely on my skill and my execution of the task at hand. For this, there could be no other excuses for my success or failure.

As for academics, I was always somewhat of a rebel. An introvert cursed with an inferiority complex; I was the one student intent on destroying the system by questioning the authority of those attempting to educate me. I often knew more, or thought I did, about the subjects taught in class than most of my so-called teachers. Worse still, I wasn't afraid to call their attention to this fact. If David was voted most likely to succeed in his class, and he was, then I should be voted most likely to start an insurrection in my class.

Why had I been able to continue this pattern of misbehavior? In part, David had established my status years ago. When I was in third grade, Jack and Johnny Miller (the twins as I called them) tormented me in nearly every way possible. And one day, I came home from school with a fat lip. Mom asked me what happened, and not being a snitch, I said I had tripped and fallen. David, however, did not believe my story, and eventually, he extracted the truth from me.

The next day, David stood on the other side of the street, hidden from sight by the bus, as he waited for Jack, Johnny, and me to exit.

Now, Jack and Johnny were in the sixth grade, younger than David but three years older than me, and they had no problem with pushing, shoving, or hitting me after the bus pulled away. That day would be no different, and as David watched from across the street, they began their daily assault on my person.

David sprinted across the street and, without saying a word, punched Jack in the mouth. Johnny tried to run away, but David pulled him down from behind by the collar of his shirt and kicked him hard in the gut. Then David pointed at the twins and shouted, "Touch my brother again, and I will fucking kill you!"

A couple of days later, Richard, the twins' older brother, went after David for retribution. David, studying to be a black belt of Shinto-Ryu training, beat the shit out of him, thus cementing my status as an untouchable.

Oh, there was a police report filed, and David got a stern reprimand, but nothing of consequence ever came of it. From that day forward, no one *ever* bothered me again. I could now do or say anything to anybody without fear of reprisal. That kind of freedom is liberating and frightening.

God's Response

I had been anxious all day, not because of school or concern about my mental well-being. That strange voice had been lurking around in my mind since that night on the beach. No, my scrambled thoughts were focused on a storm out at sea. This rare winter storm was well offshore, but its basic elements, wind, and rain, created a surfing encounter that I could not refuse.

When the final bell rang, I sprinted for the car and then raced to the house, eager to face the challenge ahead. Today, the waves could be two or three times above normal. It would be choppy as hell out there, but the chance to possibly ride fifteen-foot waves didn't present itself very often in this part of the country.

This time of year, the water temperature was usually in the mid-sixties, cold enough to require a wetsuit for any amount of time spent surfing. I never liked wearing a wetsuit; they were always such a pain in the ass to get on or to get off. By wearing a wetsuit, I also felt more vulnerable because I could not move with the speed and agility I was used to. Yet, there I was, standing in a full wetsuit, looking out at the waves with a stupid grin on my face.

What do you say, God? Can we have that long-overdue discussion now?

To my disappointment, the waves were more in the ten-foot range, not the fifteen-footers I hoped to see today. Looking up toward the sun, well where the sun should be, I could see a faint circle hiding behind the haze of the storm clouds overhead.

As I made my way to the water, I could see a few surfers one hundred, maybe hundred-fifty yards off to the right. Beyond that, there was no one else on the beach that day. No joggers, no guys walking around with metal detectors, no bikes, no one. It was intoxicating to embrace the spirit of this place, to hear the ocean's heartbeat with every crashing wave. *Hey God, anything that You would like to say? Didn't think so.*

As expected, the water was choppy as hell. Watching the surfers, I would lose track of them as they disappeared, surfing in and out of the swells. The wind swirled all around me, pushing the water up on one side and, at the same time, driving the water back down on the other. It felt like I was stuck in the heavy-duty rinse cycle of a washing machine, simultaneously moving in all directions without any rhyme or reason for the undulation.

Most surfers would paddle out toward the horizon, dipping their board below the crashing waves as they worked toward the break. Me, I preferred to swim out, the leash on my right ankle dragging my board behind me as I went. It was completely unnecessary, but as you may have guessed by now, I liked the challenge.

As always, the plan was to swim past the break, rest up for a few minutes on my surfboard, and then surf my little heart out. But today was harder; the waves were bigger, the surf rougher, and the wetsuit squeezed my body like a boa constrictor. I used every bit of strength to make it out to the break. And as my body cleared the break, I felt the tension on my leash pull hard and then go slack. I turned and looked in horror as my surfboard rushed toward the shoreline without me.

In this situation, most people would just float on their back for a while, build strength, and then bodysurf the waves back to shore. For me, oh, it could never be that easy. You see, I don't float. No, I sink like a stone, even in saltwater. I took a deep breath, looked around, and realized I was completely alone. As I had made my way out to the surf, the two surfers already out here had returned to shore and left the beach. *Okay, God, you've got my attention. What's on Your mind?*

Exhausted, I went through my options. No point in calling out for help, no one was going to hear me, and even if they did, I'd be dead by the time they made it out here. And I couldn't expect anyone to see me either. From shore, I'd certainly look like a cork on the ocean, bobbing in the sea. Now, if I could get the wetsuit off, I'd have a better chance of swimming to shore, but, as previously noted, the wetsuit was always hard to get on or to get off, and that was on land. With the churning ocean, in deep water, which would be impossible, and I'd be dead. The only viable option that I could think of was to swim.

So thus, I began my arduous journey back to salvation. Early on, I knew this was not going to end well for me, but I kept diligently trying to make it shore. Each breath of life got harder as I was tossed and turned into the sea like a drunken sailor in a tugboat. With my strength failing, my mind began to accept that this was my fate, to die like David.

Defeated, I felt my body sink toward the bottom. One last time, I looked up toward the sky. From this vantage point, I could see the sun now, a giant eye in the sky looking at me. Curious, I had not seen it all this time, but now there it was, watching me die. The eye of God, I assumed, to make sure the job was done. And then it happened... my foot hit the bottom. I grinned wickedly, with equal amounts of fear and hope coursing through my veins; I had a desperate plan in mind.

I found myself in eight feet of water, deep enough to drown me but also shallow enough to escape. I pushed off the bottom, broke the surface to breathe, and then sunk to the bottom again. In this fashion, I would pogo my way toward the shore. With every push, I floated closer to shore, and with every drop, the distance between the surface and the bottom grew shorter.

Though it felt like hours, it was just five minutes before I could stand with my head out of the water. I walked the rest of the way toward the beach and collapsed on the shoreline next to my surfboard. I began to laugh uncontrollably as I lay on my back there in the sand. I could feel the water rushing up against my body; I could smell the salt of the ocean; I could taste the saltwater in my mouth; I could hear the seagulls overhead. So, with purpose, I looked skyward but could no longer see the sun amongst the clouds.

Okay, God, message received. Sorry to have disturbed you.

Litany (Life Goes On)

Later that night, I decided to take a walk on the beach. The near-death experience was still fresh in my mind as I headed north into the moonless, starlit night. The sounds of a backyard party competed with the crashing waves for my attention, but my mind was buried in contemplating life's fragility. I could have died today, I should have died today, but here I am, drinking whiskey and cola, smoking a cigarette with the cool sand between my toes.

Someone once told me there is no such thing as coincidence; everything happens for a reason. God's will, so to speak. I never believed that fate was pre-ordained. I was content with the thought of random events beyond our control. Some good, some bad, but never dictated by a higher power. But what if I was wrong?

How do I explain the events of today? Was it divine intervention that saved me from a watery grave? Or was it just dumb luck and quick thinking that kept me among the living? And who was to say? Is it me? Is it God? Is it up to somebody reading a book in a coffee shop right now? Are the answers we seek in that very book, or is it the story itself, a story of love, regret, and the call of the great unknown, the reason we dream?

Life's a trip, Que, no?

I looked toward the vast darkness of the ocean. Distant lights on the horizon dotted the landscape, each a bastion of life finding its way in a cruel world. A strange thought crossed my mind: *It's early morning in Sidi Ouarzeg, Morocco. At this very moment, is someone standing on a beach, some four thousand one hundred and eighty-eight miles across the ocean, looking in my direction for answers?*

I smiled, lifted my drink respectfully, and said a silent prayer. First to God, then to David, and finally to that stranger across the watery abyss looking at me. What I said, or more exactly what I thought, was not important enough to record for posterity's sake. But it offered me a sense of closure and a hint of acceptance for the events that had occurred during these last six weeks.

I sat on the beach, closed my eyes, and listened intently to the waves as they crashed ashore. I could feel my heartbeat slow as the melody of the waves soothed my troubled soul. And when the haze of cluttered thoughts finally cleared, I feared the future.

All my life, David had protected, guided, and sheltered me from the misery of this thing that we call life. Now, I would be forced to face my fears, failures, and weaknesses alone. Was I strong enough to do this? Would I get caught in ticking traps? Or lose the race to rats? Would I pretend that a stranger is a long-awaited friend? Or would I build a fortress around my heart? Would I tilt at windmills when I should withdraw? And was I smart enough to know the difference between right and wrong? Left or right? Up or down?

Helpless and spiraling ever downward in this rabbit hole of fear, the cool ocean water brushing against my feet instantly sucked me back to reality. I took another sip of my drink, lit a cigarette, and decided it was time to cruise on back home.

I said home, didn't I? Never thought I could do that again.

Brand New Day

I would be up the next morning before dawn, anxious to, once again, attend my church. I would have nearly an hour to surf before I had to get ready for school. Sunrise on the ocean is a special sight; the colors bleed from the sky and into the water as the sun climbs above the distant horizon. I have seen hundreds of sunrises, and each one is a masterpiece forever etched into my mind.

The storm passed in the night, and the waves returned to normal. And, as usual, I swam my way out to the break with much better success today than yesterday's fiasco. Yeah, I'm not a big fan of failure. What's the old saying, time flies when you are having fun? Until, for whatever reason, it doesn't. I would be chased out of the water a little earlier than expected today.

As I sat there, looking for the next set to roll in, I felt a giant thud against the middle of my surfboard at the waterline. I looked down in time to see the tail of a five-foot shark thrash against the surface and then swim away. Encounters with sharks were a part of surfing, but nothing any surfer ever took lightly, especially me.

Once, when I was twelve, I was bitten by a shark. It was a four-foot black tip that got me on foot. Nothing serious, but I had a nice scar to show for my encounter. This trematode would give me a healthy respect for sharks, which would carry through these ensuing years. So, for my board to get tagged by a shark this morning, I decided it best to get out of the water.

The Avenue

School would come and go as the weekend officially got underway. Tonight, for the first time in weeks, I will go out with my friends. There was a club in town, The Avenue, that, as teenagers, we would gravitate to every weekend. Too young to get into a regular bar, the teen-oriented The Avenue would provide the perfect environment for my young angst to be exhibited.

As expected, teenage angst cannot be contained in a controlled environment, and The Avenue would prove to be no different. Technically, an alcohol-free zone, The Avenue presented the best opportunity to press the boundaries of morality and legality, and I would frequently fail on both accounts. Tonight would be no different.

Looking across the dance floor, I felt something I had never felt before. Dancing in the corner of the stage, moving with the beat of the music and oblivious to my sudden interest, she was like a Siren drawing me closer and closer to the jagged rocks. And willingly, I would go to a certain death just to feel her touch on my skin. Dirty blonde hair with a pink rat-tail stole my heart long before I even knew her name.

That night would come and go with this Angel's name still a mystery to me. Despite the liquid courage coursing through my veins, I could not bring myself to ask. I had enough problems in my life, and the thought of adding rejection to that proverbial mountain was more than I could bear.

Instead, I found comfort in the embrace of a familiar "friend." Whether out of sympathy or lust, she led me to the back seat of my car and reminded me why Prom was such a special night for us. With inhibitions and boundaries firmly cast aside, it's fun to be young, wild, and free. Unfortunately, life finds a way to fuck things up whenever it can.

Here, in the middle of such an intimate moment, I was startled to hear a knock on the window. Standing there, with a flashlight in hand, was Officer Ken. Now, Officer Ken was a real police officer during the week, but on weekends he would work security in and around The Avenue to make sure malcontents such as myself were firmly kept in check. I'm sure the double time the club paid him had no impact on his decision to spend his weekends preventing me from getting laid.

She crawled off the top of me and pulled down her skirt, hiding my consolation prize from the prying eyes of this thirty-four-year-old married father of two wearing his on-duty uniform, complete with a badge and a gun. Looking up at the ceiling of my car, I asked, "Officer Ken, can you please come back in five minutes?"

"Sorry, not how this works," he replied.

Turning his attention to the girl now sitting next to me, he asked, "Do you need assistance? Are you in trouble here?"

Embarrassed, she shook her head and crossed her arms out of frustration. She looked at me and said under her breath, "You told me this wouldn't be a problem."

Officer Ken replied, "It isn't until you get caught. Michael, you know the rules, not in this parking lot. Now, please step out of the vehicle."

"Oh, come on. Do you need to do this?" I asked.

"Yes, I do."

"Can I at least pull my pants up first?"

Officer Ken retorted, "I really wish that you would."

Once dressed, we exited my car as Officer Ken searched the interior for drugs, alcohol, and other contraband. Checking the glovebox, then beneath the seats, and, finally, in the backseat, he would not be disappointed. There, he found the last four survivors of the case of beer that my friends and I had bought earlier that evening. He began to crack each beer open, and as he poured out the golden contents on the ground, Officer Ken stated, "Michael, you've got shitty taste!"

When he was finished, Officer Ken sent us on our merry way. He left us with this tidbit of wisdom, "You don't have to go home, but you can't stay here. It's good to see you again, Michael."

We drove three blocks down the street, parked in a church parking lot, and then finished what we had started twice.

Hello, My Name is Michael

The very next weekend, my friends and I found ourselves once again heading to The Avenue. But first, a quick trip to the corner store to buy a couple cases of beer, and, as we had done so many times before, we made our way to the park to enjoy our illegally obtained libations before our rendezvous with reality.

I had many acquaintances, but there were very few people that I would call friends. But of those few, there were three who stood out far above the rest. We had all known each other since elementary school; we had all surfed together for years and were now exploring the boundaries and limitations of teenage life in a small coastal town together. We each had our unique personalities, but our differences made the group greater than the sum of its parts.

Eric Parker was the tallest and best-looking of our group. Eric was a gifted musician with dreams of seeing the world from behind his guitar. Proud and fiercely loyal, Eric expected more out of life than any one man should. But if anyone could capture that dream, it would be Eric. I wish him the best of luck in the years that come.

Paul Watson was the oldest of our group. Paul had a gregarious, larger-than-life persona. If Paul did not know the answer to a question, then he could make it up with such conviction that you would swear he was an expert on the subject at hand. Loud, brash, and egotistical, Paul was either going to be a huge success or a huge failure. If I were a betting man, and I am, then my money was on a huge success.

Alex Lee was the youngest of our group. Alex was an opportunist with a bad habit of leading with his heart and not his head. If any trouble were to start, it was because Alex had taken offense to something that was said or done; real or imagined did not matter. I worried about Alex sometimes; his Machiavellian nature, coupled with his immense passion, was just not a good combination. We always had his back, but would we always be there to save him from himself?

And then, of course, there was me. I was the quiet one in our group. Shy but extremely confident in my abilities, I was the puzzle wrapped up inside an enigma. I was never one to draw attention to myself, but I was never one to wilt in the spotlight, either. Cocky was a word that was often used to describe me, but I had always considered myself a dreamer with an attitude. I was more reserved than the others, but once provoked into action, I was a raging bull. Fearless, yet afraid of everything, I would dive headlong into the maelstrom if it meant protecting my friends from harm.

We called ourselves heathens. Well, technically, I was the one called a heathen by a street preacher when I heckled him during his soapbox sermon. It was meant to be an insult, but I, we, wore the term like a badge of honor. And when we were together, like tonight, we were a cyclone of teenage chaos just waiting to explode. After copious amounts of alcohol, bravado, and testosterone had replaced any hint of common sense among us heathens, and now we were headed toward The Avenue, God help us all.

We arrived at The Avenue just before eleven. A cursory check at the front door revealed no contraband, and we entered the establishment. I, of course, had a mission to complete, to meet that girl from last week. After a few minutes, I found her, once again, on the dance floor. Liquid courage raging through my body, I walked up behind her, and when she turned my way, I said, "Hello. My name is Michael."

What happened next was an alcohol-induced mistake, but it played a pivotal role in the months that followed. I kissed her passionately and then walked away from the scene of the crime. A few steps into my retreat, I felt my shoulder pull hard to the right. It was her, staring at me. She said, "My name is Jane."

She kissed me passionately, and I lost myself in the moment. If I had died after that kiss, then I could have died a happy man. But, as it is, life has its own plan for each and every one of us.

For the rest of the evening, I kissed her, and she kissed me. We went out to my car, and our hormones took control. When we were done, she gave me her number before leaving. The next day, I called her.

"Jane?" I asked.

"Yeah…?"

"Do you want to see me again tonight, as much as I want to see you?"

"More," she said.

I responded, "I don't think that's possible."

Shall We Make This Official?

It had been a little over three weeks now since that first night. I had met her friends, and she had met my friends. And surprisingly, we were still together. I mean, my friends can be a rich source of amusement, and a bit of an embarrassment, when a girl enters our orbit. It was certainly an acquired taste, and Jane had shown no signs of souring on their sense of humor yet.

Jane's friends, by comparison, appeared to be normal, well-adjusted teenagers. Made me wonder, where the Hell did their parents go wrong? Jane had many friends, but really one, Kim, would be considered her best friend. I liked Kim; she got me. Or to be more exact, she understood the peculiarity in me that others failed to see. I was always kind of like a duck on water; above the surface, everything looked calm, but just below the surface, chaos ruled the day.

It was a Saturday night, and Jane was staying with Kim for the weekend. Jane was sitting on the hood of my car, kissing me. I paused long enough to ask her, "What do you think about making this official?"

Jane asked, "What do you mean?"

I replied, "Do you want to date me?"

Jane said, "Of course."

I wasn't sure Jane understood what I meant, so I added, "Exclusively."

Much to my surprise, she said, "No, I like things the way they are right now."

Dejected, I responded, "Look, it's time for me to meet up with my friends; I'll talk to you tomorrow. "

Jane kissed me again and then said, "Good night."

Crushed by this rejection, I headed to the party. Once there, I met up with Alex, Paul, their girlfriends, and forty other teenagers packed into a tiny room in this big house. Paul's girlfriend, Jennifer, had a friend with her at the party. Wendy and I started talking, which led to touching, which then led to kissing. By the end of the evening, Wendy and I had found our way into a quiet part of the house, where we shared a very intimate moment in time. So, in the still of the night, I took something from Wendy that can never be undone.

I knew I was wrong to take this reward, but I had been told hours before that I was not in a committed relationship. So then, who was I to deny my hedonistic nature? However, it made me wonder what would have happened if I had just gone home that night? Life's a bitch, and so I will never know.

The next day, I got a phone call from Jane.

"Hey, look, I've reconsidered, and I would like to make this an exclusive relationship."

"Oh, fuck me," the thought echoed inside my hungover head.

Before I could suppress myself, the words just came out, "There's something that you should know about last night."

Damned If You Do & Damned If You Don't

Everyone had a week to think about what had transpired and their role in this slow-moving train wreck. And by everyone, I meant me, myself, and I. Oh, a case could be made that Jane was to blame for this debacle, but I knew better.

I, and I alone, had started down that path to disaster when I first kissed Wendy. I knew it was wrong, yet I willingly sallied onto that playing field. And I could have stopped at any time, yet I willingly rounded second and headed for third. Safely at third, I should have quit playing that game in my head, yet I willingly took a trophy I did not deserve. No, this was on me.

Having accepted the blame for this calamity, my thoughts now turned to dig my way out from underneath the wreckage I had caused. And I knew that would mean having to face Jane and Wendy.

People like to say that the important moments of your life flash before your eyes as you face death. As someone who had cheated death a few times in my short life, I had never seen such visions. That is, not until that night.

Pulling into the parking lot of The Avenue, I could finally understand why people would say such things. I relived in my head last weekend, trying desperately to undo what I had done. In this futile effort, I discovered a funny thing about the past: imperfect as it may be, it will never change. And that's hard to accept for someone who wants to change their past, someone like me.

As I exited my car, I saw Jane and Kim heading across the parking lot to confront me.

Friends, I thought to myself. *Why didn't I think of friends?*

It was Kim who spoke, "You're such a fucking asshole!"

I shrugged at her accusation; how could I argue against that point? She was right; I can be such a fucking asshole; sometimes.

"But you are going to fix this shit," she continued, "by making a choice tonight, that bitch or Jane."

Wait, I had a choice? I hadn't thought of that possibility either; I had just assumed that Jane would be making a choice for me. Ten seconds in, and already I've had to abandon my carefully crafted game plan. Oh, I am so fucked!

I needed to get away from this nightmare, but Kim was definitely not going to let me off the hook. She said, "Where do you think you're going? I want a fucking answer from you, right fucking now!"

"Look," I said, "I understand what you are saying, but I need a moment to think...."

Kim demanded, "Think about what? Pick one or the other, motherfucker."

I rounded the corner only to run into Jennifer and Wendy. It was Jennifer who spoke, "Do the right thing, Wendy gave you something that no one else could ever take, and you don't fucking care, do you?"

"Of course, I do—"

"No, you don't!" She snapped. "If you did, then this would be an easy decision for you, wouldn't it?"

The thing was, it was an easy decision for me to make; I was just looking for a way out that did not hurt anyone in the process. And clearly, this was no longer an option for me. I had felt nothing for Wendy, and I had felt everything for Jane. My decision was simple. My delivery of said decision would, however, prove to be problematic.

As if I had completely forgotten about the reason for my abrupt retreat, reality sent me a reminder when Kim and Jane rounded the corner. And so, I now found myself exposed to, and trapped between, the two sides of this bizarre love triangle.

For an innocent bystander, it must have been quite a sight to see. Two girls yelling at me, then yelling at each other, then back at me. For my part, all that I could manage was a few hand gestures and the occasional "Oh, that's not fair... No, I didn't... Please stop..."

Noticeably absent from this verbal street fight were the voices of the two people who were most vested in the outcome of this dispute, Jane and Wendy. Both silently watched on as Kim and Jennifer fought the good fight on their behalf. However, the question lingering in their eyes spoke volumes, was I worth the heartbreak or not? Personally, I would say no, but who am I to judge what is or what is not worth the heartbreak?

And then, to my horror, there was an agreement, and both Kim and Jennifer said, at the exact same time, "Make a decision!"

All four sets of eyes looked at me, and then silence.

I stood there, terrified, knowing what I wanted to say yet unable to bring myself to commit to words. What I wanted to say was, '*Please forgive me, I made a terrible mistake, and I am sorry for causing both of you so much pain. I do not deserve this chance that you give me now, and I am not worthy of your affections.*'

What I said was, "Jane... I choose Jane."

I could clearly see the heartbreak in Wendy's eyes as she silently turned to walk away. Jennifer, however, defiantly got in my face, pointed her finger at me, and growled, "You are going to regret this!"

So, as the vanquished walked away in shame, the victor, for lack of a better word, claimed her prize.

What Happened to My Car?

An uncomfortable evening was coming to an end. Jane and Kim had spent the time since my 'decision,' pretending as if nothing had ever happened. Oh, I caught Kim giving me the side-eye occasionally, but she never mentioned that train wreck. And Jane played the part of the loving girlfriend, hugging and kissing me throughout the night. Wendy and Jennifer, however, were nowhere to be seen. Part of me was relieved by their absence, and part of me was terrified.

On the other hand, I couldn't get it out of my mind. Outside, I played along with Jane and Kim, but inside, a piece of my heart died from the shame. This is not who I was, yet this was who I had become. Blame hormones if you like. Blame teenage angst if you choose. Blame parents, society, education, and modern love, and blame whomever you like. But the sad truth was this: I was responsible for this debacle.

Could I really fix this disaster? Was I up for that challenge?

I don't think so.

I tried to justify my part in this calamity internally, but the words sounded hollow and insincere in my head. And so, here I was, once again, that metaphorical duck on the water. From the outside, everything looked calm, but just below the surface, emotional chaos ruled the day. And that wicked thought once again crossed my mind: *You can be such a fucking asshole when you want to be.*

I walked Jane and Kim to the car. They had parked down the street a couple of blocks so I wouldn't see them waiting for me. I didn't think about that little bit of strategy, either. For someone who thought that he had it all figured out, I sure shit the bed on this night. I must be the dumbest or most naïve, smart person in this little town. I kissed Jane goodnight and started my way back to the Avenue parking lot.

Along the way, I tried to convince myself that this feeling of regret would pass. I could say I was happy, which would be a lie. I could say I was sad, which would be an understatement. I could say anything, do whatever, be anywhere, and it still wouldn't fill this void inside me. God, I missed David.

He would know what to say, what to do; he would know… But he wasn't here, was he? No, he left me behind. I was marooned with questions that only David could answer. If the World keeps turning, and everybody asks questions, tell me, David, what's the secret? Tell me, David, what's the answer?

Silence…only silence.

Yeah, life is but a sick joke, and by the time you figure out the punchline, your time is up in this world. I hope the punchline was worth it, David, for the humor of these last three months eludes me. Worse still, since I was now on my own, nothing could save me from the monsters lurking outside. The thought made me laugh and then sent a shiver down my spine.

I lit a cigarette, rounded the corner, and entered the parking lot from the north side. There, as if waiting for me, was Officer Ken. He put his hand out for me to stop and said, "Michael, there's something that I need to talk to you about—"

"It wasn't me. I didn't do it. And you can't prove anything." I interrupted.

Officer Ken shook his head.

"It's not that tonight, Michael."

Annoyed, I asked, "Then what is it, Officer Ken?"

"It's about your car, Michael," Officer Ken replied.

Alarmed, I dodged Officer Ken and started walking hurriedly toward my car. I felt a tightness in my chest, my pulse quickened, and my mind spun out of control. I pulled myself together long enough to ask, "What happened to my car?"

In a calm voice, Officer Ken said, "Your car is fine, Michael. Someone covered your car in shaving cream and toilet paper."

I held my hands up in disbelief, "Where the fuck were you?"

Much sterner now, Officer Ken replied, "Watch yourself, Michael. I'm not here to babysit your fucking car."

Knowing that I had just overstepped a major boundary, I immediately apologized, "I'm sorry, Officer Ken. I'm just upset; that car means a lot to me."

Slightly nodding, Officer Ken said, "That's why I wanted to find you first before you saw it. Before you did something rash."

Trying to lighten the mood a little, I interjected, "Who? Me?"

Officer Ken chuckled, "Yeah, you."

I felt better knowing that I wasn't getting arrested for my smart-ass mouth tonight, but before me was my beautiful car...defiled by vandals. "Asshole!" was written on every window, and toilet paper covered nearly every inch of red paint. I sighed and then shook my head in disbelief. Officer Ken said, "A witness said two girls did this to your car. Did you piss off anyone recently?"

I nodded my head in agreement, "Yeah, tonight."

Officer Ken continued his interrogation, "Two girls?"

"Yeah, two girls," I replied.

"Michael, I have to ask," Officer Ken began, "did you want me to file a report?"

I looked at Officer Ken; I could feel anger seeping out of my pores, "For what? Vandalism? No, I'll handle this myself."

Officer Ken shook his head, "That's what I'm afraid of, Michael."

I reassured Officer Ken, "I promise; I won't do anything rash."

Officer Ken touched my shoulder, "I hope not, Michael. In the meantime, remove the TP here and wash off the shaving cream when you get home. There shouldn't be any damage to the paint, and your car should look just fine in the morning."

I nodded, began the task of pulling off the TP, and started plotting my revenge against Wendy and Jennifer. War had just been declared, and I was never one to shy away from a fight.

War is Hell

The first casualty of the war was the relationship between Paul and Jennifer. Truth be told, it was less about backing a friend and more about stumbling upon the perfect excuse to spend more time with a mystery girl without the entanglements of a girlfriend; not exactly what you would call a moral victory, but a victory, nonetheless.

So, now what? I was new to this revenge thing and didn't know exactly what to do next. I mean, I've never intentionally set out to hurt someone. It always just kind of happened naturally. Yeah, as I have previously established, I can be such a fucking asshole sometimes. But what more could I do to girls that had been humiliated by forcing a choice, and then one losing her boyfriend for pursuing that choice?

I had no idea, but I felt it was best to avoid Jennifer and Wendy at all costs. I had decided that a live-and-let-live approach was probably the best way forward. I had won, so to speak, and now I saw no need for rubbing salt into an open wound. Oh, how naïve I was.

One week later, Jane was out of town visiting family. I, however, was still looking for a good time. Tonight would be a special night, as I would meet Paul's mystery girl, Michelle, for the very first time. We drove to a party where I expected to meet some friends. Michelle and Paul decided to stay in my car as I ventured into the party. Sex, or so it seemed, was far more fun in the back seat of my Mustang than any party could ever be. From my own personal experience, I couldn't argue with that logic.

Not wanting to know exactly what was happening in the back seat of my car, I entered the party already in progress. Once inside the house, I did not see my friends but Jennifer sitting on the couch, drinking a beer. I turned to leave, but I had been spotted, so Jennifer followed me out of the house.

I walked away as Jennifer called out to me. I pretended not to hear her voice as I made my way toward the exit. Jennifer caught up to me and pleaded, "Please, listen to me..."

I spun and threw my beer bottle in her direction. As I had planned, the glass shattered on the large oak tree behind her. I shouted, "What the fuck do you want?!"

Jennifer sighed, "I'm sorry."

I demanded, "For what?"

Jennifer lowered her gaze.

"I'm sorry for fucking with your car—"

"That is David's car!" enraged, I shouted. "Do you know how much that fucking means to me?"

Again, she pleaded, "I'm sorry."

Defiantly, I barked, "Fuck you!"

Tears began to stream down her face.

Yes, I can be such an asshole, but I have my version of kryptonite; I cannot stand seeing a girl cry. Again, Jennifer apologized, "I'm sorry."

I sighed as I nodded my acceptance of her apology.

She said, "I didn't mean it. I acted foolishly, and I hope that you can forgive me."

I didn't want to, but I found myself saying, "It's okay."

"Can I hug you?" she pleaded; eyes wet.

My defenses were completely shattered.

"Sure."

As she hugged me, she kissed me on the cheek. I pulled back, but she looked me in the eyes, tears rolling down her face.

Again, I said, "It's okay."

And then things went completely off the rails as she kissed me gently on the lips.

I pulled back and looked at her with surprise, but she leaned in and forcefully kissed me this time. I felt her kiss deep inside, and, at that moment, I lost control of myself. As if in a trance, I felt her hand place my hand under her miniskirt, and, with her help, I found my fingers inside her. I wanted to say no, I tried to say no, but my raging hormones could not resist her willing body and soul. She gently bit my ear and whispered, "Is there any place we can go?"

Unfortunately for me, there was. Not more than two blocks away from that very spot at the park which housed the ballfields of my youth. It was late; it was secluded, close by, perfect for betrayal and the many other things I wanted to do to this girl that night. I said, "Yes, there is..."

Her hand was now in my pants, gently caressing my inner beast to life. "Where?" she excitedly asked.

I nodded in the direction of the park, and with her hand still in my pants, she pulled me closer to her. She passionately kissed me, smiling, "Let's go."

We walked hand in hand toward my date with infamy. To say that I was conflicted would be an understatement. I truly loved Jane and knew this was clearly iniquitous, but the lust coursing through my blood consumed whatever virtue remained in my teenage heart.

As we entered the park, I found myself wondering, in the course of history, who would be considered the vilest of betrayers: Judas, Benedict Arnold, or myself? Judas Iscariot traded the life of Jesus for just thirty silver pieces, yet his betrayal set in motion what would eventually become the canon of the Christian faith.

A true American hero, if he had just died on the battlefield, Benedict Arnold would offer West Point to the British as he suffered indignity after indignity by political friends and foes alike. Who could blame a man of honor for wanting the recognition he deserved?

And then there was me; I was about to fuck someone because she was ready, willing, and able to do so. Love, it seemed, had no power to subdue the lust in my young heart. I had no honor, held no sacred duty, and felt no remorse for what I was about to do that night.

After careful consideration, I determined that my crime would be greater than this shortlist's historical figures. A wry smile crossed my lips as we entered the third base dugout. I've been getting away with it all my life, and now I would cross a line that cannot be undone.

So, on the bench that I had known these many years, I would fuck Jennifer, a reality that could not be ignored. The memories of my youth would soon give way to the passion she felt, the sounds I heard, and the satisfaction that emanated from my soul.

When I was done, we silently returned to the party. What had just happened was more primal than anything I had ever experienced, as it was completely devoid of emotion. I fucked her out of revenge or desire that I could not decide. But there was that voice bouncing around in my head once again, "You can be such a fucking asshole sometimes."

Outwardly, I smiled. Inside, however, I was looking for a fight with that voice, "Yeah, tell me something that I don't know."

Laughter… all I heard was maniacal laughter. The sound echoing in my mind unnerved me; I thought: *What did that voice know I didn't?*

I grabbed a whiskey bottle off the kitchen counter as Jennifer went to look for her ride. I didn't need any cola or ice. I tilted the bottle up and then drank down as much as I possibly could. When I was done, I shivered, coughed, took a breath, and repeated the process. In between gulps of amber-colored fire, I had time to think about it; yeah, that voice was right, "I'm such a fucking asshole sometimes."

Which made me wonder, "How could this get any worse?"

Jennifer was headed back in my direction now but without any friends. I had time for one more round of whiskey roulette before she reached the kitchen. She grabbed the whiskey bottle, took a swig, and said, "My ride left me; I need to get home. Can you please help me?"

Without hesitating, I said, "Sure."

We took the bottle with us as we headed for the door. As we walked toward my car, I reached for the keys in my pocket, and it hit me, *"Fuck!"*

I now understood why that voice inside my head was laughing; it was laughing at me and my stupidity. I had completely forgotten about Paul and Michelle, sitting there with my keys in the ignition, patiently waiting for me to return the car.

With no way out of this now, I kept hitting the whiskey bottle on the way back to the car. And with every gulp, I would close my eyes, shake my head, and hope this was just a nightmare. But, when I opened my eyes, I would find Jennifer walking next to me, smiling. In the middle of this disaster, she was always smiling at me.

I needed to explain what would happen a little more than a block from the car. I took a long, hard swig, looked at Jennifer, and said, "I don't know how to tell you this, but Paul, and his new girlfriend, Michelle, are in my car."

She asked, "Really?"

But the expression on her face said something different; it was satisfaction that I saw, not fear. Somehow, she knew they were there. Which meant I had been set up from the very beginning. Several random coincidences converged at this very moment as I worked to put the pieces of this puzzle together in my mind.

A mutual friend invited me to this party, and Jennifer had positioned herself so that I would see her when I entered the house. She might not have known exactly where I was retreating to, but from previous experience, she certainly would have known how to get my defenses down. Once my defenses were down, she had the skills, and the body, to take advantage of a teenage boy. All she had to do was offer up that body for my ravaging. A bargain, I suppose, to let me violate her, however, I saw fit, if the true intention was revenge. I had been outplayed, outsmarted, and now I would be humiliated, in defeat, when we got to the car.

Paul was surprised when I opened the car door and saw Jennifer standing next to me. I took a swig, put my hand to my forehead, winced, and said, "Yeah, she got left at the party, and we need to take her home."

Paul said, "Uhm, that's not a good idea."

Thoroughly defeated, I said, "I know, but she lost her ride because of me."

Confused, Michelle introduced herself, "Hi, I'm Michelle."

"I know who you are," Jennifer coldly replied.

There was that voice again, gloating now, "I told you that you were a fucking asshole."

Paul drove, with Michelle sitting in the front seat. I pounded whiskey in the back seat with an arrogant Jennifer sitting beside me. I knew the timer had been set, the fuse lit, and now I could only wait for this disaster to finally explode in my face. I wouldn't have to wait long as Paul pulled into a convenience store to buy a pack of cigarettes. Jennifer followed him into the store, and now I found myself alone with Michelle.

I broke down in tears as I explained to Michelle who Jennifer was, what I had just done, and how I had been set up for this failure. Michelle held my hand, said it would be all right, and that she would let Paul know that it wasn't my fault. In the meantime, Jennifer had pulled Paul aside and told him... everything.

Paul looked at me, shook his head, got back in the car, and drove Jennifer home. Not a word was said for the twenty minutes it took to get to Jennifer's house. The silence continued as we then took Michelle home. When Michelle got out, Paul asked, "Really?"

I offered a feeble 'I'm sorry.'

Nothing else was said that evening as we drove home.

The Aftermath

Jennifer, of course, could not wait to share with Jane what had happened between us. Understandably, Jane was not amused. Words were exchanged, I presented my case, and Jane thoroughly dismissed my protests. Things ended, as expected, with me becoming persona non grata in Jane's life.

But my relationship with Jane was not the only casualty of that night; Wendy had also ended her friendship with Jennifer. And, for some reason, Kim had ended her friendship with Jane for not giving me a second, well, third, chance to make things right. Paul wasn't speaking to me either, so I isolated myself from most of the world. How could one girl make my life so fucking miserable?

I vowed to myself that never again would I let a girl get the better of me. A heart of steel is what I would become. Yeah, that voice inside my head said, "You care too fucking much, don't you?"

I hung my head in shame as I agreed with that assessment.

So, next weekend, Kim invited me to her house late Saturday afternoon. I showed up, and it was just her and me there. I asked, "Where are your parents? Where's your sister?"

She replied, "My dad is at work, and Mom is at my sister's soccer game."

"Okay," I responded.

"Do you want to talk about what happened?" she asked.

Ashamed, I said, "No, not really."

She asked, "Can I talk about it?"

Confused, I responded, "Sure."

She hugged me and said, "I'm sorry."

"For what?" I asked.

"For Jane's reaction," she said.

I asked, "Why are you sorry?"

"Because you are a guy, so you can't help yourself if pussy gets thrown at you like that."

Really confused now, I asked, "What?"

Kim said, "You're a guy; you like pussy; I get it. Would you like to see mine?"

Even that voice inside my head was confused. I, we, had never seen Kim act, or ever speak, like that before. So, I asked a very logical question, "Are you drunk or something?"

Kim pressed her body hard against mine and said, "I want you. I've wanted you since before Jane even met you."

"What?" I laughed nervously.

Kim leaned in and kissed me.

"I want to feel you inside me/."

I was now desperately fighting that inner beast for control of my body.

"Wait... *What?*"

Kim said, "Take me now."

Yeah, I was losing that fight.

Kim took me by the hand and led me to her parent's bedroom. As she sat down on the edge of the bed, I asked, "Why are we here?"

Kim softly pushed my hair to the side of my face and over my ear. She purred, "Isn't it thrilling? The thought of doing it here?"

I hadn't thought of that before, but now that she had mentioned it, how could I not?

She crawled to the middle of the king-sized bed and gave me that come hither motion with her hand. I pulled off my shirt, kicked off my shoes, and dove headfirst into the bed, twisting in mid-air to land on my back. She climbed on top of me and took control; I always liked it when a girl took control.

When we were done, we lay there, naked, in the middle of her parent's bed. My eyes were closed now, my hands behind my head, so I shared a secret thought with that voice: "Okay, that should not have happened; but it just did."

The voice responded, "Felt great, didn't it?"

Yeah, it felt so right. Or, at least, I felt more emotionally attached to Kim than I ever did to Jennifer.

The voice, however, did not agree, "You have no fucking idea what you have done, do you?"

Kim leaned over and kissed me, first on the cheek and then on the lips. With my eyes still closed, I could feel Kim kissing her way down my chest, inching ever closer to waking that inner beast again. She took her time, and when she did finally get there, I gave the proverbial finger to that voice in my head as I placed my hand on top of Kim's head. I arched my back in ecstasy as Kim worked it to completion. I let out an audible sigh as I finished, and a wicked thought crossed my mind, "You are such a fucking asshole when you want to be."

Kim worked her way back up my body, her head landing on my right shoulder; her right arm draped over my left shoulder.

She giggled.

"That was fun!"

I smiled and kissed her on the forehead.

"Please explain to me what the hell just happened?"

She looked up at me, her eyes focused and sharp.

"I fucked you, and then I sucked you. What more do you need to know?"

I asked the only pertinent question that I could think of.

"Why?"

Kim kissed my chest.

"Because I saw you looking at Jane on the dance floor that night. You were off to the side, sitting at a table. I saw you, and I wanted you for myself."

I immediately sat up, "Then why the hell didn't you say something?"

She sighed, "I wanted to, but that move you pulled on the dance floor with Jane left me no options. She was my friend, and you obviously had an interest in her."

I continued my interrogation, "If you wanted me so much, then why did you take Jane's side when it came to what I did with Wendy?"

"I couldn't be sure if you wanted Wendy more than Jane," Kim replied with a shrug. "So, I pushed you in the direction that gave me the best opportunity to be here with you now."

I chuckled, "So you were counting on me to fuck up again, huh?"

She laughed, "Yeah. Yeah, I was."

"Okay, so now what?" I asked.

Kim looked me squarely in the eyes and stoically stated.

"I don't care what you do, I don't care whom you fuck, but you belong to me now. First, and last, and always, mine."

And that voice inside my head whispered *I told you so.*

What's Wrong with Me?

So, I now found myself in a relationship without my consent or my blessing. Kim wanted to fuck me, despite my worst behavior. So, why was I having a problem with that? I mean, what was wrong with me?

I had been given permission to pursue my worst inclinations without fear of reprisals, yet I felt wrong for taking advantage of the situation. Yes, I could be such a fucking asshole sometimes, but the real question was, why? What was hiding inside of me that consistently journeyed to the edge of morality?

The answer was always there, just beyond my grasp. I could see it in the distance, but I could never truly comprehend the meaning of what I had witnessed. So, I would turn loose the inner beast whenever given a chance.

Teenage hormones certainly played a role in this conundrum, but I could not discount other forces at work.

That voice inside my head, for example, kept pushing me further and further past the boundaries that I had previously set. In my heart, I had only ever wanted to hear the word *'no,'* but no one ever stopped me as I ventured deeper and deeper into that black hole of vanity.

Like Daedalus, I had flown into the sky, looking for an escape that would never come without a heavy price to pay. And like Icarus, I forever found myself flying too close to the sun and spiraling helplessly down into the deep blue ocean below. And Kim would always welcome me back into the fold with open arms and open legs.

Here, there be monsters of my own making. There were no rules, no boundaries, and no reasons not to push the limits of man, morality, or sex. Yet, I was trying to find reasons to limit myself in this unrestrained environment. Again, I asked myself, *What's wrong with me?*

I looked for the answer to that very question in the strangest of places, religion. As a child, I learned that there were seven deadly sins. And, as a teenage malcontent, I had found myself guilty of transgressions involving all seven. But which of the seven: pride, greed, lust, envy, gluttony, wrath, or sloth had contributed the most to my current predicament?

Pride, of course, was an early favorite. I was young, cocky, and, in my own mind, bulletproof. How could I not be guilty of pride? But, as recent events had proven, my pride, under the right circumstances, could easily be defeated. Emotionally, mentally, and intellectually, I had been thoroughly beaten by the whole world and girls alike. So, I moved on from pride to the next sin on the list, greed.

Greed was a bit trickier for me to comprehend. I had a life that provided material wealth and the actual means to acquire whatever my heart desired. Well, most of what my heart desired. Collecting proverbial scalps was more a matter of status than money spent, but I always wanted to collect more. However, this obsession was more associated with the next sin on the list, lust.

For me, lust was a big factor. That feeling of release, however brief, made me forget all about the complexities of the world. It was something so simple yet impossible to describe. My experience pushed me further and further to explore the great unknown, seeking new thrills, in new places, with new girls. Yes, lust was definitely in the lead, but there were still four other sins to address. Next up on the list: *Envy*.

Envy was a relic of the past. I had certainly been envious of David in life, but now that he was gone, there wasn't much left for me to supposedly resent. Well, that wasn't entirely true. I had to admit that I felt an undeniable bitterness toward certain girls that had crossed my path. For example, Jennifer had found her way onto a very exclusive list, but that bitterness was not enough to cause my crisis of faith. Would the next sin on the list, *Gluttony*, prove to be the culprit?

Gluttony made a brief appearance on this list as a result of my drinking. I did drink—*a lot*—but it was more about forgetting the world than changing the circumstances of my life. My excesses were partly an escape from the harsh realities that I had faced in my young life. But they were never a serious challenge to the next sin: *Wrath*.

Oh, wrath held a special place in my heart. There were lots of things, and people, that I wanted to confront. God, that fucking priest, Jennifer, the list went on and on. However, in the grand scheme of things, my anger issues amounted to nothing when compared to the problems dominating the world. For example, the Russians were in

Afghanistan, indiscriminately killing people; how could I ever match that intensity? Which, finally, left me with *Sloth*.

Sloth was just a small preoccupation. Yeah, I was lazy, but only about certain things. School, household chores, and relationships. Other things, like surfing, sex, and drinking, governed my actions throughout the day. If I liked doing it, things got done. If I didn't like it, then procrastination ruled the day. Tell me, would you have done anything differently?

So, guilty of all these sins, yet none, individually or combined, could answer the question at hand. Perhaps, I was, somehow, defective. Broken by life, was I an outcast, destined to walk these streets alone or was I an anomaly, an exception to the rule? Truth be told, it didn't really matter. I was just another flawed individual trying to make it through this thing that we call life, knowing perfectly well that no one gets out of here alive.

And there, on my desk, sat the gift that David had left me. Inside that pink unicorn wrapping paper could be the answer that I sought or the reason why I asked the question.

Either way, I needed to know the truth.

I grabbed the package and began to tear it apart. As I had suspected, it was a book, but not the book that I had anticipated. No, this was a journal and written on the cover in David's handwriting, *'I Hope This Helps.'*

The Book of David

I held the journal in my trembling hands, unsure of what to do next.

I suddenly felt constricted by the room, as if the air was being pulled from my lungs. I needed space and time to process; I wanted a drink and a cigarette. I headed downstairs with the journal in one hand, a bottle of whiskey in the other, and a pack of cigarettes in my shirt pocket.

In the gentle ocean breeze, under the pale moonlight, I sat on the sugar-white sand and lit a cigarette. Almost nothing compares to that first drag of a cigarette, absolutely the third-best experience of my short life. The top two, sex and whiskey, alternated depending upon the company that I kept at the time, but that first drag of a cigarette remained as constant as the northern star.

I fell back onto the sand, looked up at the aforementioned northern star, and exhaled. Billowing smoke rose into the night sky and was promptly scattered by the wind. And, in my head, I heard a song that I had never heard before. The melody, the lyrics, foreign but somehow so familiar.

"Remember David's smile, and the spirit moves tonight to make you shine. Remember David's words; the words he said would last all time."

I held onto the journal, with both hands, across my chest and smiled. For the first time in what felt like years, I was again at peace with the world. God, in Her infinite wisdom, had given me something that I so desperately needed now, only if I had the courage to open the book.

It seemed like a simple thing, right? Just turn the cover to the left, and the secrets contained within will be visible for all to see. And, perhaps, that was the problem. I did not want to share this, whatever it was, with anyone. I clearly wanted to keep this to myself, but the question was, could I?

It had now been a week since I first discovered this treasure, a week spent in isolation as I contemplated my next move. I went through the motions of life, but I had not really spoken to Kim, my friends, my parents, or anyone since that night. Oh, I had spoken to God and cleansed my soul in the surf, but the mortals that surrounded me were left in the dark about this conundrum.

I mean, what if David said this was a useless existence? Or something stupid, like, "I ran out of peanut butter?" How could I live with myself if that is all there is to David's story? Ah, but what if…?

It was the question that kept me up at night, the question that pushed me to pick up the journal, only to toss it down again. Fear is a hell of a powerful emotion that can propel you forward or hold you back. The problem with fear, insidious as it was, is that you never really knew which direction it would take you. That was until it took you there.

So many people proudly say that I would do this or I would do that, but everyone was a liar. The truth was, I guess it's a lot like war; you never know how you would react until that first bullet screams past your ear. Most people would shit themselves and cry like a baby, but a chosen few stand up and fire back at the enemy. I would like to think that I was one of that chosen few, but I could not find the courage to open that fucking book.

I spent hours studying the cover, hoping to gleam some truth from it, some small detail that would offer a clue to the meaning of 'I Hope This Helps.'

Occasionally, I would stick my finger under the cover as if I had finally worked up the courage to open it. Yet, I would always stop short of that one final step. It went on like this for days and days, though it felt more like years.

Eventually, when I was drunk enough and tired enough not to care anymore, I grabbed the book and opened it. There, on the page before me, in David's handwriting:

Michael

By the time you read this, I will be gone. Don't worry about me. I know exactly where I am going. And I apologize for not taking you with me, but some things you just have to do on your own. But know this, no matter where I am, I will never be more than 12,450 miles, give or take a mile or two, from you.

Listen, there are a lot of things that I wanted to tell you as you grow into being a man. I, of course, can't be there now, but I have faith in you and whom you will eventually become. I'd offer you words of wisdom, but I haven't any to share. And no, I didn't run out of peanut butter; I just got tired of this place.

I give you permission to explore all that you want in this world. Remember, the Earth can be any shape you want it... any shape at all. You, and you alone, decide your fate; not Mom, not Dad, not me.

As William Shakespeare once wrote: "This above all: to thine own self be true. And it must follow, as the night the day, thou canst not then be false to any man. Farewell, my blessing season this in thee!"

So, without further ado, I bid you goodbye. In parting, I ask but one thing of you, if you should have a son, name him in my honor. Yeah, I know that's a lot to ask, but David Alan Taylor is one Hell of a good name.

Oh, one added bonus; I've included a few extra thoughts for you on the pages that follow. The remaining pages are yours to fill as you see fit.

Love, your brother,

David Alan Taylor

The World is my Oyster

On the first few pages, David had written lyrics from a variety of songs; each one included a synopsis of their meaning to David and its relevance, as he saw it, to my life. Most of it was from bands that I had already known, but some of it was from really obscure shit that I had never heard of before. Known or unknown, all of it held a special meaning to me.

I felt so small in this place; I understood David's need to escape. I did not have the courage to follow in his footsteps, so I formulated a different plan. I would travel the country, see the sights, and hear the sounds of the world beyond this sleepy little coastal town.

Two thousand four hundred and eighty-eight miles could not be enough to soothe my wanderlust, so Route 66 and beyond would be my quest. It would be nice if your car could just tell you how to get there, but that was not how things work. No, a trip like this would take some serious planning; fortunately, I had some spare time on my hands.

Now, some people would question the sanity of what I had planned to do. After all, driving across the country alone wasn't a very practical thing to do. Dangerous even, not knowing the exact route while crossing a vast desert where everything was trying to kill you. And, if I thought about it for too long, then I would have agreed with that sentiment.

Was I nervous about taking on such an endeavor? Of course, I was. Who wouldn't be? But my need to escape the events of these last few months had consumed any lingering doubts about this course of action. I had it in my mind that, to find my way once again, I first had to get lost, both figuratively and literally. This was going to happen, whether anyone liked it or not.

The very first thing that I did was buy a big map of the United States so that I could chart my general course for this grand adventure. I spread the map out across the kitchen table and traced a route with my finger from this sleepy little coastal town all the way to Chicago, the beginning of Route 66. I used a pen to mark potential pitstops, cities like Atlanta and Nashville, and places that I had an interest in seeing along the way.

Next, I traced my route westward, again marking potential pitstops with a pen. Looking at the map, I didn't find any cities of interest to me, so I guessed how far I could drive in a day and marked those locations. Once I reached Los Angeles, I would have to decide, north or south. North, I think, up the Pacific Coast Highway to San Francisco. From there, well, I had no idea where to go next. Perhaps Alaska, or not. I'd figure it out when I got there.

Now, with a general course charted out, I took my dad's AAA card, headed down to the nearest office, and ordered a *TripTik* to Chicago. I figured once I was in the Windy City, following Route 66 West would be easy enough to accomplish. I mean, there are signs everywhere along the way declaring Route 66 West is this way. And for the next leg of this journey, once I hit the ocean, then turn right and drive north up the Pacific Coast Highway. I was told that it would be two weeks before the *TripTik* would be ready for pickup.

Next on the list were provisions. It was my intention to eat breakfast, lunch, or dinner at restaurants, diners, and roadside cafes along the way. With that in mind, I determined that I wouldn't need much food, certainly anything perishable, for this trip. I figured things like beef jerky, potato chips, and water—lots of water—would hold me over from town to town, day to day. I bought ten pounds of beef jerky, ten bags of various chips, and ten one-gallon water jugs for the trip.

For such an arduous journey, the car needed to be in good mechanical order. I took it down to the mechanic and had him check the engine, change the spark plugs, refill the fluids, and change the oil. I bought new tires, checked the brakes, and replaced the windshield wipers. Mechanically, the car was now up to the task, but was the driver?

Music would play an important role in this expedition. Not knowing what I would find on the FM dial, I made several mix tapes and purchased the albums of all the bands that David had mentioned in the journal. I bought three cases that held fifty cassette tapes and filled each one to capacity. That was more than two hundred hours of continuous music; I had hoped it might be enough.

Clothes, what to do about clothes? I loaded up two duffle bags worth of clothes for this trip. Shirts, jeans, jackets, underwear, socks, shoes, hats, anything I could think of to get me through the weather conditions I would face on this odyssey. I thought I could do laundry along the way, but then again, tossing the old and buying new might be more efficient. However, that would have to be a game-time decision, as I had no idea how this would work out in the real world.

I had no idea what scrapes, cuts, or bruises I might encounter along the way, so I wanted to be ready for whatever happened. I prepared a survival kit with the basic necessities like a toothbrush or two, toothpaste, dental floss, aspirin, and other medical supplies. In addition, I included things like a sleeping bag, a pillow, and toilet paper. For good measure, I even included multiple flashlights and batteries in the kit.

The final thing to consider was finances. How do I pay for such an endeavor? Fortunately, I am a person of means, and five thousand dollars was not beyond my means. Doing so without my parents' consent, however, was another matter. I took the money out of my parent's safe when they were not home. I know it was wrong of me, but when did right or wrong ever really apply to me?

With everything in place, I started a course of action that could not be recalled. I waited a couple of weeks before I put my plan in motion. I left a note on my bed explaining to my parents what I had done and where I was going. I didn't want them to agonize over my fate as they did with David.

It was early morning as I made my way downstairs. As I went to leave, however, I found my mom in the kitchen drinking a cup of coffee. She asked, "You're up early; where are you going?"

I replied, "Out."

"When will you be back?" she asked.

Never one to lie much, I said, "Four months, maybe more."

Mom laughed. Apparently, she thought that I was joking and asked.

"You're kidding, right?"

"Mom, I need to just get out of this town for a while," I spoke rapidly. "I feel like if I stay here, I will end up like David."

"Michael... what about school?"

Yeah, I had thought about that too.

"I spoke with my principal. I told her that I was leaving town before the end of the school year but that I wanted to graduate with my class. She checked with my teachers, who agreed that I would have no problem passing finals. Considering all that had gone on regarding David, she said she would do something unique. The grades I had yesterday would be those recorded on my transcripts.

"So," I concluded. "I will graduate with honors."

Concerned, she asked, "Where will you go?"

"North, to Chicago, and then west to Los Angeles."

Surprisingly calm, she inquired, "And then what, you will come home?"

"No," I shook my head slowly. "I was thinking about heading north up the Pacific Coast Highway to San Francisco."

"And then home?" she repeated her urgency.

I countered, "Yes, eventually; I will come home."

She stared at me momentarily, then said, "Wait here."

After a few minutes, Mom reappeared. A credit card and another five thousand dollars in cash were in her hand. She said, "For the record, I am not okay with this stupid plan of yours, but—"

"But what?" I asked.

She paused for a moment, trying to compose herself for the words that she was about to say.

"But... I've already lost one son for reasons I still don't understand."

She paused for another moment before concluding her thought.

"And I know you will find a way to do this, with or without my approval."

I nodded my head in agreement.

"I won't lose another son," she added. "At least for lack of money to survive. Common sense, maybe, but you will have enough to buy your way home if necessary. Especially with that other five thousand you took the other day."

My cheeks instantly reddened, and I felt the warmth of a blush on my face.

"You knew about that?"

She nodded, wiping away tears from her cheek.

"Take this with you," she cleared her throat but continued. "I hope this helps, but if you need anything more, just call."

Now I started to cry. I gave her a hug as she said, "Please call and let me know that you are all right. You know that I love you?"

I kissed her forehead and said, "Yes, I do."

I walked out the front door, entered the car, and turned the ignition. The car sprang to life, I put it into gear, and I left the only home that I had ever known for the open road. I looked into the rearview mirror one last time as I pulled away from the driveway. This was a sight that I knew I would not see for quite some time.

The Road Warrior

When I left town, I was excited. I was admittedly nervous, and I was definitely delusional about the ease with which this trip could be completed. I was feeling many things, but I was not truly grasping the enormity of the situation.

Oh, that realization would come later, yet in those first few moments and the days that immediately followed, I felt...free. This was an illusion, of course, but with 'The Analog Kid' by Rush bouncing around my brain, how could I not feel... *free?*

Interstate highways had made the process of traveling a long distance faster, but they had taken away any romance of the open road. It wasn't long before I found myself buying maps and looking for backroads to add a touch of mystique to the journey ahead.

Along the way, I made several stops. Though I thought that I would like Atlanta, I did not. The thing is, I could never really put my finger on why I didn't like Atlanta. It was, after all, a beautiful city teeming with friendly people and plenty of things to do. Perhaps I didn't enjoy my time in Atlanta because it reminded me too much of my hometown. I mean, every time I turned around, there was another street called Peachtree, something or another.

It was the same concept back on the coast, but everything was a variation of the word 'Beach.' Beach Road, Beach Street, Beach Avenue, Beach Boulevard, the list went on and on. I was trying to escape that place here, and all the Peachtree streets surrounding me may have been dragging those unwanted feelings to the surface. Someday, when I feel more at ease with myself, I'll have to go back to Atlanta and give it another try.

Nashville, however, was much more fun. The Grand Ole Opry was such an amazing place; the history, the music, the venue, and everything about this city spoke to me. And then getting the chance to see *A Flock of Seagulls* and *The Fixx* on the Opry stage was something that I will never forget. I could have stayed there forever, but I did have more to accomplish on this journey. With that in mind, I reluctantly headed north once again.

I made a quick stop in Louisville; I wanted to see Churchill Downs. I'd seen it on TV plenty of times, but I wanted to look out over that long dirt oval and contemplate what more than one hundred years of history felt like. The horses and all the faces may have faded over the years, victims of that fate that awaits us all, only to be replaced by something newer.

But the pomp and circumstance of a race day, the mint julep (which tastes terrible, by the way), the big hats, everything else was stuck in an endless loop in this storied place. Which is worse? To eventually die or to never change? Since death is inevitable, I would say that never changing is the worst of the two. But was I capable of change? I guess we will find out soon enough.

With my curiosity now satisfied, I moved on to the next leg of this journey.

Just a day's drive away, I finally spotted the skyline of Chicago in the distance. I would call it beautiful, but that could not really describe the city that lay ahead. Massive yet somehow compact, Chicago was everything I had imagined and more.

Looking out the observation deck of the Sears Tower, one thousand three hundred and fifty-three feet above Wacker Drive, I could see four different states in the distance. And, as a fan of baseball, I don't know how you could ever beat an afternoon at *Wrigley Field*, where I watched the *Cubs* beat the *Mets*. However, after three days in Chicago, it was now time to move on.

Heading west, I began that long drive toward Los Angeles.

With no set schedule to keep, I frequently stopped along the way. At one of those stops, I just had to see the St. Louis Arch, the gateway to the West. Situated along the banks of the Mississippi River, 'The Arch' was a symbolic representation of my journey westward. I felt it appropriate that I should mark this occasion some one hundred and seventy-nine years after Louis and Clark began their own journey west.

Moving on, I would continue my westward trek. Somewhere along the way, Springfield, I think, I began to feel that first moment of realization. Finally, things had slowed down enough for me to connect with the reality of the situation, and this extended time alone allowed me to mentally explore how I truly felt about what I was doing.

Hero of the Yesterday?

Yes, I was really doing this, and the consequences could be disastrous. A great weight fell upon me as I began to doubt my fortitude. For the first time on this journey, I felt a sense of trepidation as I drove along the highway. My internal fears were getting the best of me, and I needed something, a distraction of some sort, to keep me from falling apart.

In Tulsa, Oklahoma, I first realized that this trip should be documented for future generations. I bought an old 35mm camera in a pawn shop and began the process of photographing my way across the country. Unfortunately, that was not enough to safely put the demons of self-doubt to bed. So, I bought the first of many books in an Albuquerque, New Mexico bookstore for this trip.

I slept in hotels, campgrounds, and even on the side of the road as I traveled ever westward. For me, the stars always made the best canopy as I ventured forth upon this highway. Under their protective glow, I would use a flashlight to read the words of authors previously unexplored by me. Jack London, Ernest Hemingway, George Orwell, Charles Dickens, Anthony Burgess, the list of authors grew day by day.

By the time I reached Flagstaff, it had occurred to me that this would be my best chance to see the Grand Canyon. So, I decided to deviate from my current course west and then head some eighty-three miles to the north.

Now, I had seen many pictures of the Grand Canyon before, but none of these photographs could ever match the awe that I felt looking over that abyss from the Village. I watched the sunrise, and then I watched the sunset from the Southern rim. The overwhelming display of colors moved me in a way that I just could not explain, not then or ever since. It's just something that you simply must witness for yourself to truly comprehend.

Two things forever changed after that day. First, I knew that I could never truly capture the natural beauty on display there in the Grand Canyon with a camera, so I quit trying to photograph nature. Instead, I would focus on what made us unique: ordinary people's everyday lives. Second, I began writing in the journal, trying to paint a picture with the words at my command, which could match the sights and sounds of what I had seen, heard, and felt on the open road.

With one detour successfully accomplished, I saw no reason to pass up the opportunity to invade Las Vegas as well. So, without further ado, I forged my way toward sin city with a specific destination in mind, Caesar's Palace. Gaudy, exaggerated, and a caricature of life itself, Caesar's Palace was a living monument to everything that was Las Vegas. And I just had to be a part of that shit show.

Viva Las Vegas

Ah, how could you not love Las Vegas? With its buffets, shows, and gambling, who could forget gambling? It was a shining beacon of turpitude in an otherwise dreary desert. An oasis of sorts where you could drink, gamble, and fuck until you passed out or died.

It was early Friday night as I made my way toward Sin City. It was dark now, but I could see the shining lights of Vegas off in the distance. Like a moth being drawn to the flame, I could feel the city pulling me in. With the top down, a Waxing Gibbous moon overhead, and New Order's Temptation blaring from the speakers, I roared into the city like a conquering army.

Sailing through the traffic lights, with palpable energy radiating through my young heart, I made my way toward the promised land. As I turned onto the strip, a visual cacophony of neon lights engulfed me in its warm, glowing embrace. It was eighty-nine degrees at nine twenty-seven on a Friday night, yet I felt a chill creep down my spine as I saw the *Caesar's Palace* sign ahead.

I grabbed one of my duffle bags, the one with the money and the alcohol, and made my way to the front desk. Once there, I went to check in using my chosen nom de plume, David Taylor. Yeah, I might have liberated the driver's license of my brother on my way out the door. I didn't think that David would mind, and, in the grand scheme of things, I've done much worse things, of late, than the impersonation of a dead man. Which, by the way, turned out to be rather fortunate, considering the credit card my mom gave me to use had my dad's name on it, David Michael Taylor.

Amanda, at least that's what her name tag said, looked at the license, then the credit card, and then, finally, at me. I could tell that she had her suspicions. I got nervous as she began writing something on a piece of paper, but eventually, she said, "Welcome to Caesar's Palace, Mr. Taylor."

Amanda quickly glanced left and then right as she prepared my room key. When she was finished, she reached out and shook my hand, and in the process, she discreetly passed me a note with the key. I opened the neatly folded note, and in perfect handwriting, it said:

I get off work at midnight.

As I looked up at Amanda, she smiled.

"I hope you enjoy your time at the Palace. Please let me know if there is anything that I could do for you, Mr. Taylor."

Now, fully aware of what was happening and the risk that Amanda was taking, I quietly asked, "Twelve-thirty, my room?"

Amanda nodded in agreement, "I hope that you have a good night, Mr. Taylor."

I smiled.

"Thank you... Amanda, is it? I think that I will enjoy my time here at the Palace. Good night, and I hope to see you again."

She smiled and nodded, "Yes, me too. Good night, Mr. Taylor. Next check-in, please...."

It was a little after eleven when I finally opened the door to my room. I was exhausted, I had been driving most of the day, and all I really wanted to do was sleep. But I knew I had company coming soon, so I turned on some music, took a very long shower, had a quick shave, lit a cigarette, and then poured a stiff drink.

I sat down in the chair, put my feet up on the coffee table, hiccupped, and looked back on my busy day. I had just closed my eyes and was drifting off to sleep when I heard a knock on the door. I shook myself back to life, got up, and opened the door to find Amanda standing there in the hallway, "Hi, Mr. Taylor. Can I come in?"

I motioned for Amanda to enter, "Of course, and please call me Michael."

Amanda smiled, "Michael, I like Michael."

I laughed, "Me too. Did you want a drink?"

She nodded. I asked, "I've only got whiskey; is that all right?"

Again, she nodded. As I started to pour a glass, I asked, "Do you like it neat, on the—"

She finished the question for me, "—rocks, with a cola mixer. Can I sit?"

My attention may have been on making her a drink, but my mind was focused on that amazing body of hers.

"Yes. Please sit anywhere that you like."

When I turned to hand her the drink, I found Amanda sitting in the chair; her wavy, shoulder-length hair was now out of the ponytail she had worn at the front desk. As I sat on the couch, I said, "Thanks for the room. It's better than I deserve and certainly, more than I paid for—"

Nervously, she interrupted, "I don't want you to get the wrong idea about me. This is something that I've never done before, and I don't know what you expect of me—"

"Hey, I didn't... I don't... expect anything from you." I stopped her mid-sentence; I had to make her understand.

And, for the first time in a very long time, I actually meant it. We both took a drink of our libations, and after a pause of thirty seconds or so, I asked, "Why are you here?"

Amanda took another sip and motioned for a cigarette. I gave her one and lit it for her. I sat back down on the couch, and then she smiled as she exhaled, "You have such beautiful blue eyes, but there's a sadness in there that I can see. A sadness that I know all too well."

I had finished my drink, so I got up to make another. This one was on the rocks; no chaser needed. I sat down in my predetermined position on the couch, rubbed my forehead, and bluntly stated, "I don't want to talk about it."

Amanda leaned in towards me, took a drag off the cigarette, and then let it go, "I know that. But tell me, Michael Taylor, why are you here in a Las Vegas hotel room talking to a complete stranger?"

I snickered, lifted my glass in a toast, and said, "Because I think you are beautiful… and it beats fucking talking to myself."

She smiled and toasted back. God, Amanda had such an exquisite smile. Something about that smile made me forget, just for the slightest of moments, about the outside world. "And what about you, Amanda…?"

"Jones," she replied.

I nodded approvingly, "Tell me, Amanda Jones, what do you know about this sadness?"

Suddenly, her smile disappeared, and a sternness, the likes of which I had never seen before, replaced her cheerful demeanor.

"I know enough to know that if you let it, the sadness will consume you. It will take your soul, it will steal your reason to live, and it will leave you empty, with no emotion inside."

Nothing had ever hit me so hard as the truth in her words. I rubbed my chin and sincerely asked, "And you can help me with this?"

That exquisite smile returned as she finished her drink, "No, but misery loves company, and I could use another drink."

We spent the next few hours drinking, smoking, and talking, lots and lots of talking. I learned about her, and she learned about me. Amanda heard everything about me. From David to Jane, Wendy, Jennifer, Kim, and so on. I told Amanda everything, even the parts that I couldn't find the courage to write down on paper. The things I learned about my dear Amanda Jones:

She was twenty-four, from the middle of nowhere West 'By God' Virginia. She and her high-school sweetheart, Steve, set out for California just over four years ago. The gas money ran out in Las Vegas, so they sold the car and set up what was supposed to be a temporary home. She got a job at Caesar's Palace, and Steve worked at another Casino on the strip.

The plan was always for Amanda and Steve to move on to San Francisco. Amanda had family there, an aunt who might be willing to take them in as they sought their version of the American Dream. They tried their best to keep it together, but somewhere along the way, Steve lost his faith. One night, nine months ago, Steve succumbed to the demons haunting his mind and shot himself in the head. He held on for a few hours, but Steve died the very next day.

Since that time, Amanda had been dealing with this tragedy on her own. Oh, the people at work did what they could for her, but she needed more help than they could ever provide. So, Amanda went about her life as if everything was okay, right up until the minute that I checked in.

Amanda had spotted that same sadness in me, and she wanted to talk to someone who truly understood the sadness that she felt. So, here we were talking about lost loved ones, drinking whiskey, and, in the process, healing those invisible wounds inside our hearts.

It was well after noon when I finally woke up. The sound of knocking at the door and a voice crying out, *'Housekeeping!'* brought me back to life.

I shouted, *"Not now! Go away!"*

A curious sensation caught my attention; I could feel Amanda asleep, her head on my left shoulder, completely clothed, with her hand on my chest. The commotion brought her back to life.

"Good morning," she opened her eyes and smiled.

I smiled back, looked at the clock, and corrected her, "Good afternoon."

Amanda kissed me on the cheek, "Thank you for last night."

I protested, "I didn't do anything."

There was that exquisite smile again.

"Yes, you did. And I thank you for it."

I chuckled, "Are you hungry? I'm starving; let's order some room service."

I had started drinking again, hoping that it would cure this hangover; it did not. It was maybe thirty minutes later when the food finally arrived. As we lifted the lid off of the plate, the aroma charmed my growling stomach. If I had been alone, then I would have just gorged myself like a pack of hungry wolves polishing off an elk carcass, but Amanda's presence kept me from devouring this bounty in such a manner. So, I ate with great restraint, not wanting to frighten my dining companion. It was best to wait and see where this was going before revealing my gluttonous side to this girl.

When we were done eating, Amanda took a shower as I lay on the bed, staring at the ceiling. Almost asleep, I could hear Amanda's voice in the background.

"Hey, what are you doing tonight?" she inquired.

"Nothing... Why?"

I looked over to see Amanda standing there, completely naked, toweling herself dry.

With the towel now wrapped around her hair, and only her hair, Amanda asked, "Merle Haggard is playing tonight here at the Palace. I have an extra ticket; would you like to go with me?"

Amanda was now sitting on the couch, smoking a cigarette. She rubbed her hair with the towel one more time before throwing it at the coffee table. The towel landed as intended, but the momentum carried it across the coffee table, and so it landed in a crumbled heap on the floor. She took a drink of juice left over from room service and asked, "What's wrong with you?"

Confused, I said, "You're...."

"Naked, I know," she interrupted with a smile. "I know you've seen a naked girl before, several actually."

Amanda got up from the couch, headed over to the bed, and jumped beside me. Still very confused, I responded, "But we didn't—"

"Yeah, I know," Amanda nodded her head.

I shook my head in disbelief, "What's happening?"

Amanda sidled up to me as she assumed her sleep position and said, "Last night was a test."

I politely inquired, "Did I pass?"

She inched ever closer, "Yes, you did."

Relieved yet still tangled up in the mystery of this woman, "What was the test?"

Amanda flashed her exquisite smile, "What kind of person is Michael Taylor?"

I sighed, "A pretty shitty one, I think."

Amanda crawled on top of me, "Maybe on the surface, but I see something different on the inside. There's a better version of you, desperately trying to escape."

I didn't see it, but I was definitely beginning to feel something trying to escape. Amanda leaned in and kissed me. When she was done, she pushed her hair back with her left hand and laughed, "I can feel that I got your attention. Good."

She jumped up, got off the bed, went back to her cigarette, and asked, "Merle Haggard? Tonight?"

Now, I had heard of Merle Haggard before, but I couldn't name a single song of his if my life depended upon it. But I really enjoyed spending time with Amanda, so I resounded, "Yeah, I'll go!"

"Get up and go shower," she said, "I assume you have a car?"

I nodded, and Amanda continued, "Great! We've got places to go and things to do."

Home

It was a little after three in the afternoon when we finally pulled out of the parking lot with Amanda at the wheel. What's that, a woman driving and a man riding shotgun? Sacrilege, some would say. Well, I am no more enlightened than the next man; it's just that... she knew where we were going, and I did not.

Turning left, she asked, "What the fuck are you listening to?"

Surprised by Amanda's candor, I responded, "New Order."

She insulted, "It sucks!"

"My car, my music," defensively, I retorted.

She laughed, "Ah... no. If I'm driving, then we are going to listen to what I want."

I put my hands up, ceding the music selection to her control. She ejected the tape, turned the dial, "There, that's better."

Now it was my turn to complain, "What the fuck is this?"

She turned to face me, flashed that exquisite smile of hers, and said, "It's called Country music; get over it."

Every time I saw that smile, the outside world vanished in a haze. Oh, it would eventually come back to me, all of it. But, with each smile, it took reality longer to reestablish control over me. Back to the task at hand, Amanda said, "Oh, and by the way, I love this car!"

As we had not discussed her driving skills the night before, I asked, 'Where did you learn to drive a stick?"

Looking as if deep in thought, Amanda, perhaps, was now on a proverbial drive down memory lane. She stated, "I was driving my dad's old pickup with three in the column by the time I was twelve."

I was curious; I just had to know, "Why?"

She replied, "Because he was usually too drunk to drive, I needed to take him to the liquor store."

I laughed, but Amanda suddenly got very serious, "True story."

Wanting to change the subject, "Where are we going?"

All she said was, "Home."

The Photograph

Las Vegas, like any city, had two realities desperately trying to figure out a way to co-exist. In one reality, you had places like the strip, which, for the outsider, looked wonderous and magical. The other reality was where the people lived who made places like the strip look wonderous and magical. It was the dirty little secret that tourists were never meant to see. And pulling into Amanda's complex parking lot, I could see why the powers that be would not want people like me to see this reality.

The place was run down, an ever-present wind pushed around litter, and the people looked at me with such suspicion.

"Come on," she said as we made our way up the stairs to the third floor.

Amanda unlocked the door, and I followed her inside the apartment. She headed for the bedroom, "I'm going to get some clothes; there's beer in the fridge if you want one."

I don't know why, but I nodded my head, knowing full well that she couldn't see me. I opened the fridge, grabbed a beer, and looked around the place. It was...old. Not rundown, mind you, just old and in need of some updates. And small, my bedroom was bigger than the living room, dining room, and kitchen combined.

As I poked around the place, drinking my beer, something in the living room caught my eye. There, on an end table next to the couch, stood a solitary picture frame. It was of a boy and a girl, happy to be together in this world. I instantly recognized the girl; it was, of course, Amanda. But the boy, something about him, reminded me of someone; very nearby, I could hear Amanda coming out of the bedroom, bag in hand, as she walked up behind me. I held up the picture frame for Amanda to see, and she said, "Steve."

I studied the picture further, "He looks a lot like—"

She interrupted, "You. I know, a short-haired version of you."

Connecting the dots in my head, "Is that why?"

I could see the sadness in Amanda's eyes.

"Part of it, yes. I... I still miss him."

I had no words; I could only hug her as she softly cried into my shoulder. When she regained her composure, she pulled back from my embrace, wiped the remaining tears from her eyes, and held up her hand to let me know she would be all right.

After a couple of minutes, I could see the brightness returning to her eyes as she smiled, "But you, Michael, are not him."

"I didn't think..." I protested a little.

"Do you know how I know?" Amanda teased, and yet I had no idea where this was going.

"No."

She wrapped her arms around me, looked deep into my eyes, and, with real emotion, she whispered: "Because your blue eyes sparkle more than his brown eyes ever did."

Amanda leaned in, and then she passionately kissed me. Reality faded away as I truly felt something stir deep within my soul. She pushed me back onto the couch and took control of the pace and the order of things.

In the passion of this moment, the picture of Steve and Amanda was knocked to the floor; the glass breaking upon impact. Amanda paused for a moment, looked at the broken picture, and then resumed the program already in progress. God, I really liked it when a girl took control.

If I had died after that moving experience, then I could have died a happy man. But, as it is, life has its own plan for each and every one of us. Mine, apparently, included a date night with a girl from the middle of nowhere West Virginia to see... Merle Haggard... in Las Vegas... tonight.

What the fuck?

The Man, The Myth, The Legend

On the way back to the Casino, we stopped off for a bite to eat at Tom's Diner. Really nothing more than a hole in the wall with very good food; it was a classic diner in every sense of the word. Apparently, Tom no longer owned it, but the current management kept the name because the locals loved his food so much.

Amanda recommended the burger and fries, so naturally, I went with the club sandwich on white bread, untoasted, with chips. Yeah, I was kind of a rebel. Anyways, while we waited for the food, I asked, "Would you care to explain?"

Amanda asked, "Why?"

I nodded my head in agreement. She began, "When I saw the driver's license, I noticed the resemblance—"

I interjected, "To Steve?"

Amanda nodded, "And when I looked up at you, I saw him standing there, looking at me."

Knowing how this ended, I still wanted to hear it from her, "And then?"

"Well," she started, "I knew that was not your driver's license; I'm assuming that it belonged to your brother."

I was unwilling to let this go, so I said, "Yes, it did. And then?"

She smiled, "I took a chance."

My interrogation continued, "What was your plan?"

She looked down at the table, "My plan was to get drunk and let you do to me what you wanted."

Well, that was unexpected. I asked, "Why?"

Clearly uncomfortable with this line of questioning, "I was going to close my eyes and pretend that it was him doing those things."

Ah, I was finally beginning to understand, "You were willing to let me fuck you by pretending that I was Steve?"

Embarrassed, she nodded, "Yes, I was."

The puzzle pieces began to fall into place. "But you got scared, didn't you?"

Amanda shook her head, "No, not scared. Just surprised."

I asked, "By what?"

She said, "By you."

Confused, I inquired, "How?"

"Well," she said. "You didn't do anything; you just talked to me."

I questioned, "Isn't that what you really wanted?"

"Of course, I just didn't expect a guy to pass up the chance to."

I smirked, "I wanted to. But, honestly, talking to you, and I mean really talking, it meant much more to me than sex ever could."

She smiled that exquisite smile again.

"And when I woke up in your arms, with my clothes still on, well, that changed things for me."

"And what just happened in your apartment?" I pushed.

Amanda smiled, "That was genuine, and I meant every minute of it; with you, not him."

A realization just occurred to me, "You haven't said the name Steve; why is that?"

She looked me squarely in the eyes, "He left me alone. I spent months wondering why he didn't take me with him. I spent months thinking about joining him. And then I met you…"

I did not want that kind of responsibility, so I said, "No, no, no. Don't even—"

Amanda interjected, "It's okay; I'm not asking you for anything."

"Look," I said, "I told you everything. I'm not a good person, and you should just run away from me."

She disagreed, "What I saw last night would indicate otherwise. You might not believe in yourself, but I do."

With that, the food was delivered, and we ate in silence as I pondered my next move.

In the car, Amanda asked, "Are you okay?"

I shook my head, "No. I'm not worthy of you, and you know it."

Amanda answered, "In time, I think that I could fall in love with you."

I shook my head in disagreement, "God, please don't say that—"

"Why not if it's the truth?" she interjected quickly, desperately.

I held my hand against my forehead, eyes closed, and said, "I will find a way to break your heart."

Amanda responded, "It's already been broken; you can't do worse than he did."

"You say that now," I said, "but you don't know what I am truly capable of doing."

Nearly in tears, Amanda said, "I don't care. I will risk it all to feel that way about you."

It was nearly eight when we pulled back into the parking lot of Caesar's Palace. We went upstairs to my room and got ready for the concert. Amanda grabbed me by the hand, led me to the bed, and then kissed me; I let my guard down and succumbed to her charms. Truth be told, I thought I could easily fall in love with Amanda; I just didn't know how to make her understand that I could not be the person that she wanted me to be.

I had spent most of my life trying to convince others that I was different. And every one of them fell for the lie, everyone but Amanda. She truly understood who I was, yet she could not walk away from me. Who was more fucked up? The liar, or the person willing to believe in the liar? I leave it for you to decide.

It was now just after ten, time to work our way toward the concert. We were ushered to our seats, some six rows off the stage. And, as much as I didn't want to, I could not help but love the show. Merle Haggard had an amazing voice, and something about his on-stage swagger connected to the cultural rebellion in my heart.

When the show was over, Amanda pushed me toward the exit and shouted over the crowd noise, "Let's go!"

I leaned in and asked, "Why? What's your hurry?"

She said something, but I could not understand her, with everything going on around us. Amanda grabbed my hand and pulled me along as we finally exited the venue. Now clear of the crowd, I tried to ask again, "What's your hurry?"

Amanda looked back at me and said, "I know somebody who can get us into the after-party, but we need to get there before anyone else shows up."

Confused, "What after party?"

"For the band," was all she said.

The tumblers in my mind began to click into place, and I now understood the objective but not the execution of this plan. I inquired, "How?"

Still pulling me along, Amanda said, "We get in, we wait in the bathroom, and then, when people show up, we step out into the crowd."

Simple enough, but I was curious, "What about security?"

Amanda looked back at me, and she explained.

"Security will be checking people for entry into the party, not the people already inside."

We made it to the private bar where the party would soon happen. At the entrance was a very big, scary guy who looked at me and asked, "Amanda, who the fuck is this?"

Not rattled at all, Amanda said, "John, this is Michael, my boyfriend. Michael, this is John, head of security."

We shook hands. John hugged Amanda and whispered in her ear, "You get caught; we don't know other, understand?"

Amanda smiled, "John, who?"

We entered the woman's bathroom and took up our position in one of the stalls. So far, so good, but I was very curious how this would play out, "How long do we need to wait here?"

Amanda said, "I don't know, ten, maybe fifteen minutes."

I asked, "What do we do to pass the time?"

Amanda smiled at me and said, "I have an idea."

When she started, I laughed, "We do have to have a discussion about that boyfriend thing."

She said nothing as she went about the task at hand. I had closed my eyes in ecstasy, and the world disappeared from view as I felt that singular moment quickly approaching. After that moment reached fruition, Amanda wiped her mouth with her hand, stood back up, and whispered in my ear, "Only my boyfriend gets that. Any objections to me calling you my boyfriend?"

I shook my head. '*No.*' I may be a fool, or I may be a horrible person, but I know that act deserved some recognition beyond the standard.

"Thank you."

Shortly after, we heard the tell-tale flush of a bathroom in use. Amanda looked at me and said, "Now's the time."

We opened the stall and walked out; the very confused young lady washing her hands looked up as Amanda wiped her mouth again for emphasis and said, "Yeah, I did that."

We exited the bathroom and walked directly into the party, which was just getting underway. Twenty-five people or so were already standing around, drinking, smoking, and otherwise milling about. Amanda and I looked over at John, who gave a subtle nod to let us know that we had succeeded in infiltrating the party. Amanda kissed me on the cheek and said, 'I love you."

Out of obligation or true emotion, I could not determine which, I responded, "I love you, too."

It would be another twenty minutes or so before the band made their way to the bar. There was a thunderous round of applause as Merle Haggard and the band entered the room. Amanda had gone to the bathroom actually to use the bathroom this time. I, on the other hand, sat at the bar.

Merle walked up, sat next to me, and asked. "What are you doing here?"

Unfazed, I responded, "Drinking whiskey, and you?"

Merle smiled at me, "The same."

When his drink arrived, I raised my glass in a toast and said, "Here's to whiskey, women, and song. In no particular order."

"Amen to that!" Merle added.

I laughed as I finished the drink and then asked, "What about another?"

Merle asked, "Seriously, why are you here?"

About that time, Amanda exited the bathroom and was actively looking for me. I pointed over to Amanda and asked Merle Haggard, "Do you see her?"

He said, "Yes."

I chuckled as I said, "Apparently, she is my girlfriend and loves your music. I would do anything to make her happy."

Amanda came up and kissed me on my cheek; she sarcastically asked, "Who's your friend?"

Merle nodded to me, "Now I understand. What's your name, friend?"

I responded, "Michael."

"Michael," he said, "Don't fuck this up."

 "I don't intend to."

Merle laughed, "None of us intend to, Michael; it just happens,"

I stated, "Amanda, this is Merle Haggard. Merle, this is Amanda Jones."

Merle kissed her cheek and said, "I've heard so much about you."

Leaving Las Vegas?

It was close to six in the morning when Amanda and I stumbled our way back to the hotel room. I didn't remember the details of how we got to the room. However, I did remember that it involved laughing, lots and lots of laughing. I didn't remember opening the door. I don't remember what happened after we entered the room, and I certainly didn't remember going to bed. Yet, there I was, in bed and naked, when the phone rang.

Slowly, very slowly, I picked up the phone.

"Hello?"

The voice on the other end said, "Good afternoon, this is your two o'clock wake-up call."

I hung up the phone, laid back down, and sighed, "I don't remember asking for that."

Amanda, also naked, stretched and then rolled over so that her head rested on my shoulder.

"I did; I have to work at three."

I ran my fingers through her hair, "I feel like shit."

"But you don't look half bad," she looked up at me, smiling. "I guess I'll keep you."

With my eyes still closed, I smiled, "How kind of you."

Amanda kissed my chest, got up, and went about getting herself ready for work. I, on the other hand, went back to sleep. Before leaving, she jumped on the bed to wake me again, "I get off work at midnight."

I nodded in agreement. She kissed my cheek and then left. I heard the thud of the door, rolled over, and then drifted off to sleep. It was just after five when I woke up again. It had been nearly twenty-four hours since I had eaten, and my stomach was complaining about the absence of food. I got out of bed, grabbed my jeans lying on the floor, put them on, and then made myself a drink.

There, on the bar, were several instant camera pictures lying about. I don't remember any of those either. One of the pictures was Merle Haggard and me; written on the back of the picture was:

Whiskey, women, and song. In no particular order.

—Merle Haggard

Another picture was an extreme close-up of Amanda's face, her left hand holding back her hair and her exquisite smile emanating from the picture. On the back of this picture, it said:

Michael, don't fuck this up.

—Merle Haggard

There were other pictures as well, but I needed food before I could try to piece it together last night. I showered, then went downstairs to grab a bite to eat. When I was done, I walked through the check-in area and discreetly blew a kiss at Amanda. She smiled and nodded as I passed her station.

Needing a drink, I headed to the closest bar. I sat down, ordered a Jack, and waited for my reward. I suddenly heard, "Hey, do I know you? You look familiar."

I turned to look and realized it was the young lady from the bathroom last night. Not wanting to get entangled in that mess, I said, "I don't think so."

She smiled and said, "Yes. Yes, I do. You're the guy in the ladies' bathroom last night."

Completely busted, I replied, "Oh, that was you?"

Still smiling, she asked, "Are you in the band?"

Noncommittal, I replied, "I can neither confirm nor deny that I am in the band."

She moved in closer and said, "I can do better than she did last night."

I responded, "I don't think so."

She purred, "There's only one way to find out."

"Look," I said, "I'm good, but thank you for the offer."

She asked, "Where is she?"

Trying to avoid this complication, I said, "Waiting for me in the room."

She said, "We can go to my room, and she will never know what happened."

I shook my head, "But I would. And that is enough for me."

She smiled, "You have no idea what you are missing."

I nodded in agreement, "Three days ago, I would be willing to find out. But today, I can't."

I grabbed my drink and headed for the Casino floor. The person that I previously was would have never passed up such an opportunity, yet here I was, thinking about Amanda. What the Hell was wrong with me?

As I walked, I hit the Casino floor, the sights and sounds echoing in my head. I played Blackjack, Poker, Roulette, and, eventually, Baccarat. Yes, Baccarat; if it was good enough for James Bond, then it was good enough for me.

Gambling is not an exact science; it is more of a feeling than anything else. And tonight, I had that feeling. In just over five hours on the Casino floor, I had racked up just over ten thousand dollars in winnings.

I looked at my watch, and it said eleven forty-eight. I cashed out my chips and headed back to the room. At twelve eighteen, I heard the lock click, and Amanda walked in.

"How are you?"

"I won some money tonight," I smiled. "So, I'm doing just fine. And you?"

She jumped up on me, the momentum spinning us around as we ended up falling on the bed. She said, "Better, now that I see you."

Amanda kissed me, "I missed you."

"I missed you too." I smiled.

She did that thing again, and it felt just like it did in the bathroom stall; nothing could beat that feeling, that emotion, as I surrendered my heart and soul to her, and she willingly accepted all I had to give.

It was now four in the morning, and I was up smoking a cigarette, looking out the window over the city. It was either really late or very early, depending on your point of view. Yet, the city was still teeming with life. Amanda woke.

"Are you okay?"

I nodded and said, "You know that I am supposed to leave for California in a few hours."

Amanda got out of bed, came up behind me, draped her arms over my body, kissed my neck, and whispered, "There's something that I have wanted to ask you, but I just don't know how."

I laughed.

"Funny, there's something that I want to ask you too."

She said, "Then why don't you just ask?"

I shook my head, "Ladies first."

"What if you stay here with me? I have the apartment; we could live there together."

I put my right hand on her left, "Or, you could come with me."

She asked, "What?"

I said, "Come with me to California."

"I can't," she protested.

"Yes, you can. If you want to."

Amanda begged me for understanding, "And then what?"

"I have no idea. I just know that I feel better with you than without you."

"Me too, but I can't just leave."

"Why not?" I spat out quickly, countering.

"I have a job... I have responsibilities..."

"To whom? Or what?"

She retorted, "I don't have much money; how will we pay for things?"

"Don't worry about that. I have a little over eighteen thousand dollars in cash right now. I think we'll be all right."

"Eighteen grand? Where the fuck did you get that?"

I smiled, "I told you that I won some money tonight."

Stunned, she said, "I thought you might have won a couple hundred or something; how much did you win tonight?"

Still smiling, I said, "Just over ten thousand."

Doing the math in her head, Amanda asked, "Wait, you walked into this place with eight thousand dollars?"

I nodded.

Amanda asked, "Why didn't you tell me this before?"

I replied, "Would it have made a difference?"

She responded, "Yes, it would have. How much did you take to gamble with last night?"

I wasn't really sure of the relevance, considering the financial windfall that had come my way, "One thousand."

Amanda shook her head in disgust, "You're such a fucking idiot!"

Very confused, I said, "But I won big; what's the problem?"

"Because..." she cried. "Most people don't... he didn't win."

It finally occurred to me why Amanda was so upset with me, "Wait, are you telling me that Steve took the last bit of the money and gambled it away, hoping to win big?"

She nodded her head as she wiped away the tears rolling down her face. I went to hug her, but Amanda pushed me away. I tried again, but she still pushed me away, just not as hard this time around. On the third attempt, however, I was successful as she finally gave in and softly sobbed into my shoulder for a couple of minutes.

When she regained control of her emotions, she declared, "If this is ever going to work between us, you are going to have to let me control the money from now on. Do you understand?"

I wasn't sure exactly what had just happened, so I asked, "Does this mean?"

Still wiping away the tears, she said, "Yes, I'll go with you."

I hugged Amanda and then went to kiss her. She put her finger up to stop my advance on her lips, "But, we are going to do this my way. Do you understand?"

I nodded in agreement. Amanda said, "No, I need to hear you say it."

I sheepishly looked at the ground and muttered, "We will do this your way."

Amanda smiled, "Now, was that so fucking difficult to do?"

I shook my head and then leaned in for a kiss. Our lips met, and fireworks exploded in my mind as Amanda pulled me onto the bed.

The Plan (As Determined by Amanda)

When we were done with our celebration of sorts, Amanda decided that I should stay in the hotel for one more night. So, she talked to a friend at the front desk and had my departure date moved back by one day. It wasn't until later that I figured out she just needed the extra time to get rid of Steve's shit before I could step foot in the door.

Amanda was up by ten, took my car, and ran the "errands" that she had to do for the day. She insisted, rather bluntly, that I stay in the hotel room and get some sleep while she was out. I slept for a couple more hours, got up, and then ordered room service.

About twenty minutes later, there was a knock at the door. I opened the door, fully expecting much-needed food. Instead, I saw John standing in front of me.

Surprised, I said, "Hey, John! Sorry, I was expecting room service… what are you doing here?"

Stoically, he stated, "Yeah, room service is going to be a little late with your order. We need to talk."

I opened the door further and invited John into the room. I asked, "Do you mind if I make myself a drink first?"

He shook his head and entered the room. He reminded me of a proverbial mountain, standing there towering over me. Trying to break the ice, I asked, "So, John, did you play football? Because you are a really big guy."

Straight to the point, "I played Defensive End in college, could have gone Pro, but I blew out my knee in senior year."

That did not make this any less uncomfortable. Out of bravery or stupidity, I never knew which; I asked, "So, John, what can I do for you?"

He replied, "What are your intentions with Amanda?"

He didn't look mad or emotionally unstable, but I was beginning to truly fear for my life. I mean, Amanda was an extremely attractive girl, and there were no way other men wouldn't develop feelings for her. And if she turned down this guy, for me? Oh shit, was he here to kill me out of jealousy? I was very nervous, and it must have shown in my voice as I asked, "What exactly do you mean?"

Sensing my distress, John said, "No, it's not what you think. I'm not here to hurt you... yet"

I let out an audible sigh and put my hand up to my heart.

"Thank God! Wait, then, why are you here?"

John once again asked, "What are your intentions with Amanda?"

I didn't know the right answer, and I was still afraid that the wrong answer might provoke a physical response. I went with my honest take on the subject at hand, "John, I don't understand what you mean."

John said, "Michael, may I sit down?"

I replied, "Please do."

John sat on the couch and said, "Let me try it this way. Michael, I've known Amanda for a long time. And in that time, even with Steve, I have never seen Amanda happier than she was the other night with you."

Even sitting down, John still scared the shit out of me.

I replied, "Look, John... I have no idea what that girl wants. Hell, I don't even know what I want. I was just passing through town on my way to California."

John said, "That's what I wanted to talk to you about."

Curious, "What does that mean?"

John leaned in towards me, "I know that you were supposed to check out this morning, but Amanda changed the checkout date. And I want to know, why?"

Not sure what I should or shouldn't say, I replied, "Because I wanted to stay another night?"

John said, "I don't think so. It is my responsibility, as Amanda's friend, to protect her from people who might harm her. When Steve died, I went to every fucking apartment in that complex and told everyone that if they ever hurt Amanda in any way, they would have to deal with me."

Terrified again, I protested, "John, I don't know what the fuck you think, but I have done nothing to hurt Amanda."

John smiled, "I would have broken you in half by now if you did."

That comment did not help my anxiety level any, but John continued, "Look, Michael, management knows about the other night. They are not amused."

Genuinely concerned, I asked, "Is Amanda in trouble because of what I've done?"

John shook his head no, "They don't know about you yet, but she will be in some trouble because of what she's done. Someone saw her crashing the party the other night and reported it to management. Michael, I want to ask you to do something for me."

Nodding my head, "Sure, John. What did you want me to do?"

John looked me in the eyes and emphatically said, "Take Amanda with you when you leave."

Confused, I asked, "What? Why?"

John responded, "They are, most likely, going to suspend or maybe even fire her for the other night. Amanda has a chance for real life if she can only get out of this town. She won't leave on her own, but I think that she would leave with you."

Humbled by his request, "I would take her."

"You *must* ask her. If she says yes, then please take her with you. If she says no, we both did our best to help her in a difficult situation."

I nodded in agreement, "And what if I already did? And what if she already said yes?"

John stood up and shook my hand, "Michael, then you are a good man."

I said, "Truth be told, I am not. I have never been whom I wanted to be, and I have never wanted to be who I am. But I am trying, and that, alone, should count for something in this world."

John patted me on the shoulder and said, "It does to me, and it will to Amanda."

John left the room, and so now it was just me, trying to figure out how I got to this point and where this would go from here.

Room service would eventually arrive, I would eventually eat lunch, and Amanda would eventually return to the hotel room just before two. She walked in the door and handed me a bottle of Jack, a pack of cigarettes, and a lighter. She said, "I don't give a fuck what happens tonight, but you do not leave this room before I get back. Do you understand?"

I nodded and asked about dinner.

"Room service, motherfucker," is all that Amanda had to say.

She kissed me and said, "I get off work at midnight."

It was about twelve-thirty when Amanda finally opened the door. After drinking for more than six hours, I was completely trashed by that point. I smiled.

"Hey!"

Amanda asked, "How drunk are you?"

I held up a bottle of Jack that was more than half gone and replied, "This much."

She shook her head, "Asshole…."

I asked, "What?"

She replied, "Nothing. Here's the plan, tomorrow you check out and move into the apartment with me."

I shook my head no, "I don't want to stay in Las Vegas."

Amanda smiled, "It's not for long, just a couple of weeks while I wrap up some loose ends here."

To be completely honest, I said, "Your apartment complex scares the shit out of me. I'd rather stay here…."

Amanda looked me in the eyes, "Here, it will cost more money. There, nobody will fuck with you or your car."

Confused, I asked, "How can you be so sure?"

Amanda smiled, "Because I went to every apartment and told them if they bothered you, or your car, that they would have to answer to John. Frankly, no one wants to answer to John."

I smiled, "Yeah, I know what you mean."

Not amused, Amanda asked, "John was here?"

I nodded. Amanda asked, "What did he want?"

Not sure how to respond, I said, "For me to take you away from Vegas."

"He really asked you to do that?"

I replied, "Yeah, scared the shit out of me in the process... but yes."

She laughed, "I always knew that he was a sentimental fool... never thought that he would ask you, of all people, to take me away from this place."

"What the fuck does that mean?"

Amanda smiled, "No offense, but you are hardly the respectable type."

"You see," I said, "That's what I told him. John still said that I was a good person."

"You are. You just don't see that in yourself."

I replied, "I don't, but I am trying."

Amanda kissed me, said goodnight, and then I passed out shortly thereafter. In the morning, I checked out, and then we made our way to her apartment. When we arrived, things looked different than before. For one thing, the broken picture on the floor was gone. Other things had changed too, but I did not want to pry. Amanda had her reasons, and I had mine.

The next day, as we lay in bed, Amanda said, "I don't need you to be happy."

"I know…"

She inquired, "Then why are you here?"

I replied, "Because I love you."

She smiled, "Ah, you're such a fucking asshole sometimes, aren't you?"

"You have no idea."

So, when she went to work, I spent my time reading books and writing. When she came home, we would have sex, and then she would take an interest in my day. I shared with Amanda the books I was reading and the things I had written. She followed both with equal enthusiasm, yet not quite understanding why it meant so much to me.

She would always ask, "What does this have to do with anything?"

I would always answer, "Absolutely nothing, and positively everything."

Amanda sketched things; I wrote things. I could not draw as she did, and she could not write as I did. Amanda painted with colors, and I was learning how to paint with words. Both talented and yet, very different on so many levels.

There was no judgment or shame in how we expressed ourselves. We were both artists, better than ordinary street rats, each with a different talent. These differences could prove to be our undoing, yet they could bind us together in a way that mankind could never understand.

Three weeks after I left *Caesar's Palace*, Amanda and I finally hit the road for California.

The Pacific Ocean

During my time with Amanda, I developed a tolerance, however slight, of Country Music. In fact, there were a few Country artists that I truly enjoyed. Obviously, Merle was on that short list, as well as Johnny Cash, Reba McEntire, Dolly Parton, and Waylon Jennings. However, my absolute favorite Country artist was Willie Nelson. I felt it appropriate to play "On the Road Again" as we left Las Vegas, heading southeast toward Kingman, Arizona.

Some might ask, why Kingman? And it would be a fair question to ask, as it would seem to be a counterproductive detour if our first destination was Los Angeles. Yet Kingman is where I deviated off of Route 66, and I was still determined to drive all two thousand four hundred and forty-eight miles of this storied road. We made our way into Arizona and then headed west again as we resumed the journey already in progress.

It was nice to have a traveling companion, someone to talk to, someone willing to do a certain thing for me, her boyfriend, to break up the monotony of the open road. There wasn't much to see on this part of the journey. I mean, for me, at least, the landscape looked foreign and oddly beautiful, but there was a shortage of civilization here in the small corner of the country. It looked and felt as if time itself had simply forgotten about this place and just moved on.

A little over two months ago, when I first started this journey, I couldn't wait to be alone, on the open road, with just my thoughts to keep me company. Now, I found myself afraid to be alone, on the open road, with just my thoughts to keep me company. It wasn't hard to figure out what had changed since then. But it was difficult to truly comprehend just how much I had changed in such a short period of time.

Sometimes, the universe opens itself up, and in a moment of true consciousness, you have just seconds to decipher the mysteries of life. You try as hard as you can to hold on to that knowledge, but eventually, you will have to blink. And when you open your eyes again, it's gone. It's the shortness of life that always leaves you wanting more, even when that bright light calls you... home.

I wanted to go home, I needed to go home, but there was something that I had to do first. There was something mysterious, something dangerous, something wonderous calling out to me from the West. Every fiber in my being longed to see, touch, and to savor the Pacific Ocean.

We stopped for the night just outside of Los Angeles, in Barstow, California. We ate at a greasy-spoon diner, hit the corner liquor store for more whiskey and cigarettes, and then headed back to the hotel for the night. Once there, we drank and smoked, we laughed, and we made plans for the next day. Santa Monica Pier would be our first stop, and then a quick trip over to Venice Beach.

It was well past noon when we finally woke up. We ate at the same greasy spoon from the night before and then headed toward the pier in Santa Monica. We walked along the pier, hand in hand, as we went to the edge and looked out, over, and into the great Pacific Ocean. A feeling of tranquility came over me as I beheld the vast sea that laid out before me. Far beyond the horizon, I could feel the allure of the Hawaiian Islands calling my name.

Next, we headed to Venice Beach. A crush of humanity walked, skated, biked, and otherwise moved across the sidewalks surrounding the beach. It would be here that I would see my first Pacific Ocean sunset. The colors exploded across the sky as the sun retreated ever westward. And at that moment, I truly understood the natural beauty of California.

We headed back to the motel for more whiskey, cigarettes, and sex. To my complete satisfaction, for Amanda and me, everything always ended in sex. It was fun to be young, wild, and free. Yet it couldn't last forever; the young part, that was.

We, well actually, I, found out that David Bowie would be playing the Forum in a week. I could not, in good conscience, miss that show. Amanda could care less, but I was emphatic about this point, "It is David Fucking Bowie!"

So, we stuck around town, visiting things like Rodeo Drive, the Hollywood sign, and other mainstays of this massive city. When the time came for the show, we waited around outside the Forum and bought a pair of tickets from a scalper. We paid three hundred dollars for two seats, the twentieth row, dead center of the stage.

It was, by far, the best three hundred bucks that I had ever spent in my life.

Bowie was a monster on stage; he consumed the oxygen in the Forum as the audience gasped and screamed for more. Amanda, however, met his performance with an atypical "meh" as she watched the mayhem unfold. I understood it wasn't Country, and she just didn't understand the importance of this performance. I, on the other hand, was losing my fucking mind.

When the show was over, and with the music still ringing in my ears, we made our way back to the hotel. Once there, we started drinking again. Amanda asked, "Did you enjoy the show?"

Smiling and still high on the adrenaline of the show, "Fuck yeah! Didn't you?"

She smiled that exquisite smile of hers, "All that matters to me is that you enjoyed the show."

I laughed, "How could you not like Bowie?"

She asked, "How could you not like George Jones?"

I replied, "I've heard of George Jones, but I have no idea what songs he sings..."

Amanda exclaimed, "Exactly!"

Then it hit me, Amanda had heard of David Bowie, but she didn't really know who David Bowie was before tonight. Yet, she suffered through this concert just for me. I said, "I love you."

Amanda replied, "Obviously, I love you more."

San Francisco

The next day, we left the city of angels and headed north along the Pacific Coast Highway. Our next destination on this journey of self-discovery was the great city of San Francisco. Founded by Jose Joaquin Moraga Francisco Palou just days before the Declaration of Independence was signed, San Francisco had always been an intriguing enigma to me.

It seemed that, from my remote vantage point on the Atlantic coast, San Francisco was, somehow, always the answer and always the problem to the identity crisis that was constantly consuming America. It seemed as if anything was possible within the confines of SF, yet the laws of the human jungle still applied to the Golden Gate City. And now, I would finally get my front-row seat to the petri dish that was San Fran.

Not more than a long day's drive from city to city, we decided to make several stops along the way. We had the time; we had the money, so why not make the most of this adventure. We ate, we slept, and we drank whenever the opportunity afforded itself. We stopped in places like Santa Barbara, San Luis Obispo, Monterey, and Santa Cruz.

The California coast was truly an amazing place. The variations in landscape, weather, and the ever-present Pacific Ocean all combined to form this magical experience. It was, of course, just a façade. If you looked close enough, you could see the cracks forming on the edges of society. As these fissures moved inward, they devoured anything that stood in their way. And from what I had seen, the only thing that could save you from this terrible fate was money.

The thought that I, with my family's wealth, could flourish in this place, yet people like Amanda would be led to the proverbial slaughter; well, it made me sick. Amanda was a far better person than I could ever hope to be, but her financial reality made survival in this environment impossible. I had always understood that money gave me the opportunity to be the fucking asshole that I had become, but I was just beginning to realize how a lack of money could keep people like Amanda from reaching their true potential. That realization was progress for me, or so it would seem to be a step in the right direction.

By the time we reached Davenport, I was sick of this state. I had grown weary of the harsh realities that were always on display but never discussed openly among mixed company. Of course, all that changed when we finally entered San Francisco. Once inside, moving from district to district, I understood why people would risk living in this city.

We made our way to the address that Amanda had been given by her mother so many years ago. Her Aunt Julie was, at some point in the distant past, living in this modest house some halfway up the hill. I asked, "Are you ready for this?"

A very nervous Amanda said, "No, I definitely am not."

I replied, "Are you sure that you want to do this?"

Amanda nodded, "Yes, I am. Do you want to know why?"

I said, "Sure."

She smiled, "Because you are here with me at this moment."

We walked to the front door, and Amanda rang the doorbell. She grabbed my hand hard as we waited for some kind of response. About a minute later, we could hear the lock open, and the door swung slightly ajar, "Can I help you?"

For Amanda, the recognition was instant. However, for Aunt Julie, time moved somewhat slower. Excitedly, Amanda cried, "Aunt Julie, it's me... Amanda!"

At first, Aunt Julie looked confused, but eventually, that confusion gave way to the realization of who was really standing there on her little porch. But I could tell this wasn't a welcome surprise, yet Aunt Julie enthusiastically asked, "Amanda? Is that you?"

Amanda, emotions running extremely high, said, "Yes, it is!"

They hugged for a minute or two. Afterward, Aunt Julie looked at me and asked, "Steve?"

I held out my hand and said, "No, I'm Michael."

Aunt Julie shook my hand and stated, "You look a lot like Steve."

I smiled, "So I have been told."

Amanda took Aunt Julie's hand, "Steve didn't make it. Michael helped me get here."

The conversation went on for several minutes as Amanda and Aunt Julie went from years past until the moments of today. However, what Julie was saying, and how she was saying it did not match up with the fear I saw in her eyes. For the objective observer, her aunt had the look of a trapped animal desperately looking for a way to escape. It was a look that I was extremely familiar with, having felt that same way when I was caught between the two warring tribes just a few months ago.

Amanda, of course, was oblivious to whatever was vexing Aunt Julie. Standing on the outside of this emotional circus, I noticed that Aunt Julie was reluctant to invite us into her home.

What's inside that she doesn't want us to see? I wondered to myself.

Eventually, Amanda asked, "Can we come in?"

Completely aware that something was amiss, I watched as that fear exploded in her eyes. Aunt Julie politely said, "Of course."

It wouldn't take long for me to determine the source of Julie's anxiety. From the other room, a woman's voice asked, "Jules, who was at the door?"

A few seconds later, this other woman appeared from what I assumed was the living room. She said, "Oh, I didn't know that we had company."

Aunt Julie responded, "Jan, this is my niece, Amanda, and her boyfriend, Michael. Amanda and Michael, this is my roommate... Jan."

Jan graciously replied, "Oh, hi! Nice to meet you!"

But I saw a flash of anger in Jan's eyes, something that I had seen in Jennifer when I announced my decision to choose Jane over Wendy. This, obviously, was a source of tension, and certainly not the first time that this conflict had come up between these two women. And I now understood why Aunt Julie had left the middle of nowhere West Virginia for a place like San Francisco.

So, for the first time in my short life, I had found myself as the only person in the room who completely grasped exactly what was happening, and now I contemplated my next move. For some odd reason, I decided that the truth, no matter how uncomfortable it could be, was the best way forward. Well, that was certainly out of character for me, wasn't it? When the timing felt right, I said, "It's not my place to tell Amanda, but I will do that if you want me to."

I saw the fear start to dissipate in Aunt Julie's eyes as she said, "No, that won't be necessary. Amanda, Jan is more than just my roommate; she's my... girlfriend."

Amanda had the look of a child who had just found out that Santa Claus wasn't real. It was always a traumatic experience, to be sure, and you would lose that childhood innocence in the process. But, in return, a whole new world of possibilities would open up around you. Amanda looked to me for confirmation of what she had just heard. I nodded in agreement, I leaned in and then whispered into Amanda's ear, "People love whom they love; there's no rhyme or reason to it. Otherwise, how could anyone explain why you would love someone like me?"

I watched as the pieces of the puzzle fit together in Amanda's mind.

"Ah, that would explain a lot," Amanda smiled.

Aunt Julie sighed, "I imagine that it would."

I didn't have the heart to tell Aunt Julie that Amanda's epiphany had nothing to do with the living arrangements or sexual orientation of her and Jan.

The four of us had dinner in the dining room of this cozy little house halfway up the hill in San Francisco. We drank, we laughed, and we talked about the world we lived in and life in general. Aunt Julie learned about how Amanda and I first met, the cross-country journey that I was on, and the whereabouts, but not the sordid details, of Steve's demise.

It was towards the end of dinner when Jan asked us if we had a place to stay while we were in San Francisco.

"No, but that won't be a problem," I replied passively. "We have plenty of money, and plenty of choices, at our disposal."

Yet Jan insisted, and Aunt Julie agreed, that Amanda and I should stay there, in this cozy little house halfway up the hill, while we were in town.

The Plan

(As Determined by Aunt Julie)

We spent days exploring everything that San Francisco had to offer. Fisherman's Wharf, Alcatraz, the Golden Gate Bridge, Chinatown, and we even drove down Lombard Street. We walked through Haight-Asbury, Russian Hill, and Nob Hill and took the time to ride the cable cars. We spent our time trudging up hills and pacing ourselves down hills. Yet, tourism can only last so long, and we had the decision to make: do we stay, or do we go?

I knew that Amanda's original plan was to stay, but a lot had happened in the years since that decision had been made. We hadn't discussed exactly what to do next, so I had to ask, "What do you want to do?"

Amanda replied, "Whatever you want to do."

No, no, no…" me not accepting that as an answer. "You don't get to drop this decision in my lap. You, and only you, need to decide what we do next."

Amanda asked, "What do you want to do?"

I put my head in my hands, "What did I just say to you?"

In a moment of honesty, Amanda said, "I don't know what to do. Part of me wants to stay, and part of me wants to go. What do you want to do?"

I said, "This isn't about what I want; this is about what you want. I understand how you feel, truly I do. And I know that it would be easier just to let somebody else make this decision for you, but I will not be that person."

It was well past midnight as I sat alone on the patio, drinking whiskey, smoking a cigarette, and looking up at the stars. Amanda was fast asleep as Aunt Julie ventured out into the cool, crisp night air. Aunt Julie asked, "So, Michael, what are you two going to do?"

I took a drag of my cigarette and slowly let it go, "I don't know."

Julie said, "You know, we all thought that Amanda went to Nashville; none of us expected her to end up here."

"That would make sense," I agreed.

"But Tammy, Amanda's mom, asked me to deliver a message... if Amanda happened to show up here."

I looked over at her and asked, "What was the message?"

Aunt Julie smiled, "Come home, just come home."

"What would you do? If you were Amanda?"

"Amanda isn't like me. There's no reason for her to stay here in this city."

"What is so different?" I asked. "Your sexual orientation? Or her desire to escape West Virginia?"

"It's different for girls, who like girls..."

"That may be true, but you do have an opinion on this subject, and I'd really like to hear it."

"I will share my thoughts with you about that subject," she replied and countered. "But first, I want to know more about you, Michael."

I pointed at my chest, "Me?"

She smiled, "Yes, you."

I shrugged, "Sure, what do you want to know?"

"Who is Michael Taylor?"

I chuckled, "Well, the answer to that question would depend entirely upon whom you ask."

She pushed for an actual answer, "I'm asking you, Michael. Who are you?"

I sighed, "So, do you want the truth? Or would you prefer that I say what I think you should hear?"

Aunt Julie replied, "The truth if you please..."

I took a swig of whiskey, "The truth... *my* truth isn't easy to explain..."

"The truth never is." she smiled.

I let out a big sigh, took another drink, and followed that with a drag off my cigarette. When I exhaled, I began.

"The truth is, Aunt Julie, that I am not a good person."

She countered, "Why would you say that?"

I shook my head in shame, "I've done terrible things."

"We've all done terrible things, Michael. It's human nature; we just can't help ourselves. The true test is in what you do after."

I laughed heartedly, if not nervously.

"I ran away. I lied to myself and others, saying that this trip was all about self-discovery. In truth, this trip was about me escaping."

She leaned in and probed, "Escaping from what, Michael?"

I had never bothered to define what, exactly, I was running from...until that very moment. Ashamed, I said, "Me."

"Michael," she said, "There's no shame in wanting to run from the worst parts of you. In fact, I'd be concerned if you didn't..."

I looked down at the ground, "I could run a lifetime and still not find the forgiveness that I need."

"What forgiveness, Michael? And from whom do you seek this forgiveness?"

I was really exploring that deep, dark place that I had always wanted to avoid. I started, "Every terrible thing that I have ever done, and from everyone whom I did it to."

She took my hand in hers and said, "You have to be able to forgive yourself, Michael, before you can seek the forgiveness of others."

Tears were now rolling down my face; I pleaded, "*How?* How do I forgive myself for the things that I have done? Things that are not forgivable?"

In a reassuring voice, Aunt Julie said, "It comes with time, Michael. Patience and time."

"I'm fresh out of patience, and time will catch up to me soon enough."

She smiled, "This is terrific progress, Michael. But I sense something more... there's something else that you are trying to run from as well."

I was now shining a light on that dark corner of my mind, the place where fear and loathing had staked a claim. And I found something there, something... unexpected. Aunt Julie inquisitively pushed me onward.

"Did you find it, Michael?"

I nodded. She asked, "What is it, Michael?"

I shook my head; I did not want to answer that question. Aunt Julie pressed on, "What is it, Michael? What do you see?"

I was still shaking my head no, yet Aunt Julie was relentless, "Tell me, Michael, what do you see?"

Feeling trapped, "I don't want to say it."

"You can't address what you are running from, Michael, if you cannot say it aloud."

I was still shaking my head *'no'* when she finally broke down my defenses.

"Michael, it's Amanda, isn't it?"

Sobbing, I nodded my head in agreement.

"What about Amanda?" she asked soothingly.

The ramparts had been breached, and there was no fight left in me; I confided, "I'm afraid that I will hurt her."

"How would you hurt Amanda?"

I smiled, "Someone once told me, 'Don't fuck this up, Michael.' But that's all I have ever done... fuck things up."

She requested, "Is Amanda aware of the things that you have done?"

I nodded, "I've been completely honest with Amanda about... everything. All of it."

She pried, "Even this fear of... 'fucking things up'?"

"Especially that fear."

"What does Amanda say about this fear?"

I was still smiling weakly.

"That I cannot do anything to hurt her."

Curious, she asked, "Why is that?"

Somewhat aloof, I responded, "Because Steve had shattered her heart. Amanda said that I could never do anything worse than what Steve did to her."

"I sense some hostility... are you angry with Steve?"

I nodded, "Of course I am."

Genuinely interested, Aunt Julie inquired, "Why? You never even met Steve."

Just the mention of his name, and I could feel the anger rising from below.

"Because *Steve* left Amanda when she needed him most. He took the coward's way out and left her all alone to face this world."

"Am I to understand that Steve committed suicide?" she pushed forward but with gentle tones.

I nodded.

"How does that make you feel?"

"For him, nothing at all," I shrugged. "For Amanda? I feel her pain. All too well, I feel her pain."

"How do you feel her pain?"

I shook my head in disbelief; I was actually going to say the quiet part out loud.

"My older brother, David, also committed suicide."

Aunt Julie pressed on, "In the same manner?"

"No. Steve took the gun, and David decided to drown himself in the ocean."

"Have you spoken to a professional about David's death?" Aunt Julie inquired sincerely.

I shook my head.

"Why not?"

"I wouldn't even know where to begin..." I laughed.

"At the beginning, it's always the best place to start."

I nodded in agreement as Aunt Julie mused. "Do you know what I think?"

I shrugged my shoulders; I genuinely had no fucking clue. She continued, "You are trying to protect Amanda from a pain that's already happened... to both of you."

I had to ask, "What can I do?"

"Well, to start, you need to understand that what you are trying to do is impossible."

Curious, "How so?"

She thought for a minute before she spoke.

"You cannot undo the pain of the past. The best that you can hope to do... is learn from it, identify the causes of it, and then move on from the pain."

In a candid moment, I confessed, "I'm not good enough for Amanda... I never will be."

"That's not for you to decide. That is for Amanda to decide. And by everything that I've seen, she believes that you are more than good enough."

"But I don't want to hurt her."

Julie leaned in and smiled.

"None of us intend to hurt people, Michael; it just happens. Nobody's perfect. We all make mistakes, Michael. That's a part of life, a part of love, and a part of relationships. The true test is in what you do after."

I smiled and nodded in agreement. For just a brief second, the universe opened up to me, and in a moment of true consciousness, I found myself staring at the great mysteries of life. I tried to hold on to that knowledge but eventually had to blink. And when I opened my eyes again, it was gone.

"You asked about my thoughts on what you and Amanda should do?"

I nodded. Aunt Julie said, "You should take Amanda to Nashville. She's a country girl, and it is the one city in this country where I think Amanda would be truly happy to live."

Then it dawned on me that this, all of it, was just a test. I smiled.

"Your advice depended on what I just said, didn't it?"

She nodded, "Of course it did. I'm a psychiatrist; this is what I do for a living. I delve into people to find out what they are made of and then help them find a way forward in this world."

"So, there is some hope for me?"

Aunt Julie laughed.

"There's always hope for everyone. But you, Michael, are a far better person than you give yourself credit for...and for me, that is all I need to know about you. Good night."

She went back inside the house, and I stayed a little while longer, looking at the stars and thinking about what had just happened.

The Plan

(As Determined by Me)

Amanda was up well before the smell of coffee roused me from my slumber. I stumbled out into the kitchen to find Amanda waiting there with two cups of coffee. She smiled that exquisite smile of hers as she handed me a cup, "Good morning, sunshine!"

I nodded; the drink of last night was still heavy in my head. Instinctively, I held the coffee up to my nose and breathed heavily to catch that delicious aroma. I opened my eyes and asked Amanda, "Have you made up your mind yet?"

Amanda took a sip of coffee, "No, I haven't."

I replied, "What do you think about going to Nashville?"

Amanda yawned and scratched just below her right ear, "Why Nashville?"

Recalling what Aunt Julie had said to me just a few hours ago, "Because you are a country girl, and I simply cannot think of any other city where you might be so…happy."

I could see the wheels turning in Amanda's precious head. She pushed her hair up and away from her face and smiled, "I like that idea."

I had to ask, "Is that a yes?"

Amanda put her left hand on my right cheek, looked me squarely in the eyes, and whispered, "Yes."

I could not be sure if it was the coffee, or something else, that was producing this warmth emanating from my body. If I had died after that look, then I could have died a happy man. But, as it is, life has its own plan for each and every one of us. Mine, apparently, included driving this girl from the middle of nowhere West Virginia, across the country, to Nashville. What the fuck?

We stayed with Aunt Julie and Jan for another week as we mapped out our route to the East. I had suggested that we should see some of the natural and manmade wonders, such as Yellowstone and Mount Rushmore, that conveniently stood between here and Nashville. Doing so, however, would require us to take a less direct route, one that would add more than a week of drive time to the journey.

I had been on the road for nearly four months now, so I saw no harm in taking another detour. Amanda, however, just wanted to get there and start her life over again. After careful negotiation and the clever use of my tongue, I was able to "convince" Amanda that the memories of this specific detour would be worth whatever time we lost in the process.

When it was time, we said our goodbyes to Aunt Julie and Jan. Aunt Julie hugged me and whispered, "Remember, none of us intend to hurt people, Michael; it just happens. Nobody's perfect; we all make mistakes. That's a part of life, a part of love, and a part of relationships. The true test is in what you do after."

I nodded my head in agreement as those words firmly took root in my mind. I realized that I was a flawed individual, one who would always mess things up, but after, it would have to be different. I was trying to do things differently, and that alone should count for something in this world.

Right?

As we made our way Northeast, we stopped in places like Sacramento, Reno, Mill City, Carlin, Wells, Jackpot, and Pocatello. Each night, we would eat, then drink and smoke until early or late, depending on your point of view, into the morning. Once awake, we would have sex, eat at the nearest Diner, and then move on to the next stop. Eventually, we ended up in West Yellowstone, Montana. It was from this hole-in-the-wall outpost that we would venture out and into the park.

We would see rivers, waterfalls, and a massive lake. We would see bison, elk, and the occasional bear as we roamed the boundaries of the park. We watched as Old Faithful spewed water some two hundred feet into the air. We walked among geysers, witnessed the glory of Dragon's Breath, and saw the splendid colors of the Grand Prismatic Hot Spring. We were both awed and humbled by the theatrics of it all. Mankind might be the dominant species on this third rock from the sun, but Mother Nature still ruled this world.

Welcome to Cody, Wyoming

(I Hope They Kill You)

After a week of Yellowstone, we moved on, ever Eastward. The next morning, we found ourselves in Cody, Wyoming. Named for the famous William Frederick "Buffalo Bill" Cody, this shithole of a city offered the only motel for miles and miles around.

During this part of the journey, I let Amanda take the lead. After we left Reno, Amanda drove a lot of the time, and she dealt exclusively with the locals. Standing in the background, I had pulled my hair up, tucked inside a trucker hat, so that I did not stand out amongst the ordinary folk that dominated this region of the country. Things were going as planned until that fucking morning.

As we waited for our breakfast, Amanda and I drank coffee. Four cowboys, some three or four years older than me, stopped at our table on their way out the door.

The leader of this motley crew asked Amanda, "Why are you with this asshole?"

Not missing a beat, Amanda retorted, "Because he's got a very big dick. But you wouldn't know about having a very big dick, would you?"

His friends laughed at him, but he noticed the position of the hat and pulled it off my head. As my hair fell into its natural position, he asked, "Who the fuck are you?"

Not wanting any trouble, I responded, "Someone who is just waiting for his breakfast, that's all."

Incredulously, he asked, "Are you one of those, them there, new wavers?"

Again, trying to diffuse the situation, I said, "I'm just an individual if that's what you mean..."

Defiantly, he erupted, "I hope they kill you!"

Obviously, a line had been crossed, and I needed to respond to this challenge. In a low, menacing voice, I made my stand, "Yes, they probably will... after I kill your fucking ass!"

Not wanting to face the odds of a four-on-one fight, I continued, "And two of your friends too: the third walks away with a permanent limp so that everybody knows what I did here. I leave it to your three asshole friends to decide which two of you die and which one lives."

Silence, it always ended in silence. Sensing that I had the advantage, I continued my quiet rampage, "I'm hungover, and I'm less in control of my anger issues right now, so in thirty minutes, I will be standing outside this diner... if you want to die, then be there waiting for me. Otherwise, shut the fuck up, and get out of here!"

Thirty minutes later, I found the local Sherriff waiting for me outside of the Diner. He said, "Son, we need to talk."

It was at this point that Amanda spoke up, "Then it's okay for the locals to threaten outsiders like me?"

Taken aback, the Sheriff said, "I don't know what you mean."

Amanda glanced my way and then quickly winked as she continued her tale of misery, "Those four assholes threatened to rape me. My boyfriend stepped up to protect me from those animals...and now you want to protect those locals?"

Clearly, on the defensive, the Sheriff said, "That is not what I was told."

Amanda said, "Yeah, I doubt that the truth would be a part of what they had to say."

The Sheriff said, "Wait... are you saying that they assaulted you?"

Amanda responded, "Verbally, yes. Then they threatened to do things that would, in most states, be considered rape. Is Wyoming one of those states? Or is the threat of sexual assault just considered normal behavior for the locals?"

It was the Sheriff who was now looking for an escape, "No... I don't think... are you sure?"

Amanda continued, "Is threatening to fuck me, and make my boyfriend watch, part of your local's vernacular?"

The Sheriff stated, "No, that's not acceptable behavior."

Amanda continued, "Well, that's what they threatened to do."

The Sheriff still protested, "I didn't know."

Amanda pounced, "Then you had better figure out what the fucking locals are trying to do to girls like me."

In the middle of Amanda's performance, the waitress had stepped out of the Diner and onto the sidewalk. She wiped her hands on her apron, then pulled out a cigarette and lit it. She walked up to the spectacle, already in progress.

"Hi, Bob," she said with recognition.

The Sheriff tipped his cowboy hat and replied, "Hi, Carol."

Carol asked, "Is this about what happened in the Diner?"

The Sheriff nodded, and Carol continued.

"Tommy started it. Johnny, Mark, and Billy were with him."

The Sherriff asked, "What did you see?"

Carol replied, "They were on their way out, but for some reason, Tommy stopped."

The Sheriff continued his investigation, "What did you hear?"

Carol took a drag off of her cigarette and then exhaled.

"I didn't hear the initial exchange, but I did hear Tommy say, rather loudly, I hope they kill you…"

The Sheriff asked, "Then what happened?"

Carol took another drag, dropped the cigarette to the ground, and crushed it out with her shoe, "About a minute after it began, Tommy and the boys left. Tommy looked angry, but Billy looked really scared as he walked out the door. I assume that's why you are here, not Tommy and the boys."

The Sheriff played with the whiskers on his chin as if deep in thought. He slowly reached out and pulled the hat off my head. My hair, once again, fell down to its natural position as we waited for the Sheriff to make his decision. Would it be a day in jail for me or a day on the open road?

"Son, when are you leaving town?" the Sherriff spoke to me directly.

"We were heading back to the hotel to check out when you stopped us," I responded.

Sheriff again tipped his hat to Carol, "Thanks, Carol."

Carol nodded as she headed back to the diner. The Sheriff turned and looked at Amanda, "We are going to pretend that none of this ugliness happened today."

Amanda nodded as the Sheriff turned his attention back to me, "Son, you really need to get a haircut if you are going to be in this part of the country for long."

The Sheriff handed me back my hat.

"Safe travels then, and don't ever come back to Cody, Wyoming. Do you get my meaning, son?"

I nodded, put my hat back on, and quickly made our way back to the hotel. We went upstairs, packed, and left town as soon as possible. Amanda jumped into the driver's seat, looked over at me, and smiled.

"Well, that was fun!"

I laughed, "Let's not do that again... at least, not anytime soon."

Amanda fumbled around, looking for a specific tape. Once she found it, she put the cassette in the tape deck, started the car, and then spun the tires as we left the parking lot. The soulful sound of Waylon Jennings' 'Luckenbach, Texas' played as we put Cody, Wyoming, forever in the rearview mirror.

Finally able to relax, I leaned my head back, closed my eyes, and smiled.

The Kansas City Scuffle

With the "Cody Showdown," as it would eventually be called, behind us, we moved east, spending the night in Buffalo, Wyoming. Buffalo was, more or less, another Wyoming shithole. Buffalo, just like Cody, had been labeled "historic" by somebody, at some point, long ago in the past. One man's history, however, was just another man's trash; such was Wyoming to me.

Granted, my opinion of Wyoming was certainly jaded by what had happened in Cody. And, to me, historical meant a building just twenty-five years old, not these turn-of-the-century relics that lined Main Street. Perhaps, I had misjudged the Cowboy State, but I had done so with good cause.

The night in Buffalo was, thankfully, an uneventful experience. The next day, we slept in, checked out late, and grabbed a bite to eat at a local Diner. We were again on the road to Mount Rushmore at about half past three.

Hero of the Yesterday?

The sun was setting as we pulled into Custer, South Dakota. Determined to press on, we made a left and drove further into the Black Hills. But nighttime in the Black Hills was far darker than any night I had ever experienced. Unable to see and completely alone, we eventually saw a shimmering light in the distance.

Amanda turned the car into the hotel parking lot, I inquired about a vacancy, and some twenty minutes later, we found ourselves in a room. A hot shower, a kiss goodnight, and blissful sleep; who could ask for anything more after another long day on the open road?

The following day, we made our way to Mount Rushmore. You could briefly see the massive faces jutting out into that blue sky above as we rounded a turn in the road. We parked, then walked down the Avenue of Flags. There, before us, were the faces of George Washington, Thomas Jefferson, Theodore Roosevelt, and Abraham Lincoln carved in stone—iconic Americans, every single one richly deserving of this great honor.

Thanks to American History class, I could recite who these men were and their place in our country's history. I could tell you about the order in which they held the office of the President. I could tell you about when they were born, and you'd be informed about the roles of

George Washington and Thomas Jefferson in the American Revolution, the explanation of the importance of Abraham Lincoln, and his famous Gettysburg Address. I could even discuss how Teddy Roosevelt led the charge up San Juan Hill in Cuba.

Yes, I could recite, convey, voice, and inform you about all of these things and more; but what I can't do is relate to any of it. I know *about them* but lack the wisdom to understand *why* this should matter to me. I assume that an understanding would be discovered as necessary to appreciate these men at some point in the future. One day, when I do, I will write down on paper what each man means to me; until then, let me enjoy this moment's beauty.

We stood there, completely in awe of this monument. The faces of granite, the blue sky overhead, and the flood of people washing over the grounds. How could you not feel the power of such a sight? Yet, as with anything that glorious, the moment passed so quickly that I almost missed it.

By noon, we were in Rapid City for lunch. By dinner, we were in Bonesteel, South Dakota. In the morning, we moved Southeast to Omaha, Nebraska. From Omaha, we continued until we reached Kansas City. It was early afternoon as we entered the city, and I felt comfortable in my surroundings for the first time in a while.

We checked into the hotel and sought out entertainment in the civilized world. At some point, we settled into a bar a couple of miles down the road from the hotel. We drank, free of the restraints placed upon me by the country we had driven through, in a place that felt more comfortable.

We were drinking whiskey and shooting pool in this neighborhood bar, not caring about the world outside of this intimate space. I was ordering another round from the waitress while Amanda lined up a shot on the pool table. When my back was turned to the table, this guy walked up behind Amanda and tried to lift her mini skirt, "Let's see what you're hiding, honey."

Amanda quickly turned and slapped his face; her anger filled the room, *"Fuck you, asshole!"*

I heard the rage in her voice over the low din of the bar, so I turned around and found Amanda standing face-to-face with this stringy-haired, shabby-looking guy. As I surveyed the scene, I could see her right hand balled up into a fist, ready to strike. With defenses in place, I was fully prepared for a fight.

"What happened?"

Without ever breaking eye contact, Amanda said, "This asshole tried to lift my skirt when I was taking a shot."

The guy turned to me, hands in the air, in a sign of submission.

"I didn't know she was with anybody," he attempted to explain away his shitty manners.

I picked up Amanda's pool cue from the table, barely in control of my anger.

"Now, you do. And you had best get the fuck out of here before I beat you to death with this!"

The guy, again with his hands in the air, said, "I'm sorry."

He turned and started to leave the bar. That, apparently, was not enough for Amanda as she shouted, "Fucking pervert!"

He walked out the door, turned right, and then disappeared into the night. Meanwhile, the entire bar had come to a complete standstill, watching this drama unfold. When the door shut behind the scruffy pervert, the place sprang back to life.

A man at the table next to us moved a few feet in our direction and said, "Some people are assholes."

I nodded as Amanda barked, "Rack 'em!"

It was a little after ten when we left the bar and headed for the parking lot. The lights overhead gave off a weird yellow glow that gave this place a sinister feeling. Amanda must have sensed it, too, because she gripped my hand even tighter as we walked toward the car. I surveyed the lot for any signs of life, but the only thing that I could see was a cat walking across the wall at the far end of the lot.

Then it happened.

From behind the dumpster, that same greasy asshole from the bar a couple of hours ago lunged forward and punched me in the face. I saw it coming, but it was already too late to prevent the blow. He caught me on the right cheek, just below the eye. It was a solid hit but not the knockout blow that he had hoped for.

Dazed but not out, I fell to the ground as I struggled to regain my senses. There, laying on my right side, I opened my eyes to see a piece of lead pipe about two feet long, with an elbow attached at one end, underneath the dumpster. I reached in, pulled out the pipe, and braced myself for what was to come next.

I turned to see him on top of Amanda, his left hand at her throat; his head turned toward his right hand, which was desperately trying to get under her miniskirt. I heard him say, "Let's see what you're hiding, honey."

Standing in striking distance, I growled, "Hey!"

He turned to look at me as I swung the pipe as hard as I could. While he may have missed his target, I did not. The blow squarely struck his mouth, teeth and blood splattered across the weird yellow glow of the parking lot lights. The impact pushed him off and to the right of Amanda. I looked down, and I could see the fear in her eyes and the blood flowing from her nose.

I had heard of the expression, blind rage, but until that moment, I had no idea it could ever apply to me. I stepped over Amanda, looked down at the piece of shit lying on the ground in front of me, and I felt that rage consume me like a bonfire. I truly wanted this motherfucker dead as I swung the pipe again and again.

On my third swing, Amanda grabbed my arm with her right hand and took the pipe from my grasp with her left. That fear was still in her eyes, but she said, "My turn."

Amanda swung the pipe down and struck him hard.

He whimpered, "Please stop...."

Amanda hit him again, "That's what I said, motherfucker!"

As Amanda wound up for her third strike, a coup de gras between his legs, she mockingly said, "Let's see what you're hiding, honey!"

Amanda wiped the blood from her nose and spit at the now unconscious would-be rapist. I pulled her so that we were face to face.

"Look, we've got to get out of here, now!"

We headed for the car, and I took one last look behind. He was still unconscious, but I could see his chest moving up and down as he involuntarily wheezed for breath. We threw the piece of pipe in the trunk and then left the parking lot.

Amanda looked over at me from the passenger seat and asked, "Did we kill him?"

I shook my head, "I don't know."

Still wiping the tears from her face, "I hope so."

Back at the hotel, we lay on the bed, and I held Amanda tight as she softly sobbed. I could do or say nothing that would make this right. I just ran my fingers through her hair and whispered in her ear, over and over, *I love you.*

After an hour or so, she looked up at me and said, "I need to know."

I nodded my head in agreement, grabbed the keys, and headed back down to the scene of, for lack of a better word, the crime. When I arrived, there were no police, crime scene tape, or reporters taking pictures. The only thing that hinted at the violence of that night were a handful of teeth strewn about, a pool of blood, and a blood trail leading off into the distance.

We left at five in the morning, eager to put Kansas City as far behind us as possible.

What Happens Next?

Neither of us had much to say as we moved ever Eastward. When we reached the Missouri River, I stopped the car, opened the trunk, and tossed the pipe into the great abyss below. Getting rid of the pipe, the only piece of evidence that could definitively link us to the horror that was the night before, almost made it feel like it was just a bad dream... almost.

In the hours that followed our departure from Kansas City, I had time to reflect upon my life and what had happened since I left home; I had time to reflect upon why I left home. The pieces of the puzzle might have fallen into place, and I, possibly, began to understand what all of this meant to me, but why it meant anything at all still eluded me.

More puzzling to me was my emotional outburst in that parking lot; why did I want to kill that piece of shit? Yes, he had attacked Amanda, and that, in itself, should be enough; but it was something more than that. In under a year, my life went from being perfect to fucked up in the blink of an eye. And though I didn't start this course of events, I was certainly responsible for most of what had happened in the time since David's death.

You are what you do, and I have done terrible things. Either out of anger, out of spite, or out of fear, I had done terrible things. Simply because I could, because I wanted to, or because it was easy, I had done terrible things. I had left to escape this pain, yet somehow, I had found something more valuable than I ever thought possible, and still, I had done terrible things.

It was in this moment of reflection that I found myself emotionally naked and afraid. Could I be the person that I truly wanted to be? Or would I always be the person that I was today?

Feeling completely alone, I asked Amanda. "Who am I?"

Amanda laughed, "My boyfriend."

I shook my head, "Who am I, really?"

She looked at me, "My boyfriend; that's all I need to know."

I stated, "Then, you know that your boyfriend is an asshole."

She smiled, "Yeah, I knew that. I still love you anyway."

I asked, "But what if... one day, I hurt you?"

"I know that you will find a way to fuck this up," she shrugged. "I also know that I will always love you."

I stated, "I don't deserve this."

"Of course, you don't, but it's not up to you now, is it?" Amanda giggled.

"You deserve better than I can ever do."

"True..." Again, she smiled. "But no one will ever love me as you do."

Everything that I had ever felt, everything that I had ever feared, everything that I had ever hoped for...vanished with those words. I was exactly where I was supposed to be, and time, no matter how cruel it would be, could never take that away from me.

In the distance, I could clearly see the Gateway Arch high above the horizon. And at that moment, it dawned upon me that I had come full circle while on this journey, for it was here, months ago, that I truly set out alone, looking for answers. It was fitting that it should end here, with a girl from the middle of nowhere West Virginia still looking for answers. The thought of the irony, the symbolism, and the absurdity of it all; just made me laugh on the inside. I must have been laughing on the outside as well because Amanda asked, "What's so funny?"

I shook my head and said, 'Welcome to St. Louis."

We checked into a hotel and then headed to Gateway Arch. I had walked through the Arch one way on my journey west, so I decided that I should walk through the Arch the other way on my journey east. It seemed fitting to me; I mean, I left here, one person, and then I returned, a different person.

Time and experience are the only things that separate us from who we were yesterday and who we are today. And a lot of time had passed since I had been here, and experience, well, I had quite a few along the way. Was I a better person for the time and experience? I don't know, but I was trying, and that should count for something in this world.

We went back to the hotel, and I just lay there looking up at the ceiling.

Amanda asked, "Are you okay?"

I nodded, still deep in thought about my journey and what I had become along the way. Certainly, I was not the same person who left this town, but I returned very much the same. The difference was obvious, but the explanation for why I had returned was a bit more complex. It appeared that Amanda had touched me much deeper than I had ever anticipated.

As I fell asleep, I dreamt of a world where none of this mattered. But, in the end, everything mattered. I could only do so much to save myself from myself. And I could do only so much to save Amanda from myself. It's funny how that worked; the best of intentions always gave way to reality.

In the morning, I awoke and kissed Amanda on the forehead. For better or worse, I was here, looking toward a future that I did not deserve. Yeah, life wasn't fair, but neither was the alternative. And, if given a choice, I would always choose life over death.

Nashville

From St. Louis, we made our way toward our ultimate destination: Nashville. Along the way, we stopped at a small Diner for lunch. The waitress looked at me and asked, "What happened?"

Looking up from the menu, I said, "What?"

The waitress pointed to her right cheek, "What happened?"

I had forgotten about the massive bruise on my cheek, but it was quite obvious that other people couldn't help but notice it.

"Oh, I got into a fight," I said passively.

The waitress continued, "And the other guy? How does he look?"

I let out a wry smile, "Worse."

Still interested in my bruise, the waitress asked, "What did you fight about?"

I nodded my head in the direction of Amanda, who was so buried in the menu that she didn't even hear the conversation between the waitress and me.

The waitress looked at Amanda and stated, "Some things are just worth fighting for."

I looked at Amanda and smiled, "Yes. Yes, they are."

It was at that very moment Amanda finally looked up, "What?"

I waved my hand and shook my head.

"Nothing. What do you want to eat?"

Amanda, with both elbows on the table, stared back at me, smiled, and then rested her chin on her hand.

"I'll have the burger with fries."

The waitress looked over to me, "And for you, slugger?"

I laughed, "The same."

The waitress turned and walked away. When the waitress was safely out of earshot, Amanda asked, "Slugger?"

I laughed, "Yeah, you should really pay more attention to what's going on around you. She asked about my face."

Concerned, Amanda inquired, "What did you tell her?"

I shrugged, "The truth."

Amanda demanded, "How much of it?"

I shook my head, "Just the part about a fight and how it was for you."

Amanda suddenly got very serious, "I never did thank you for that."

I smiled, "Yes, you did. This morning when you did the thing that I like so much."

Amanda wiped her mouth with her hand for emphasis and smiled, "Yeah, I did that."

We ate lunch and talked about the final leg of this journey. In a few short hours, we would be in Nashville. Up until this point, it had just been a dot on the map, but very soon, this would be our reality. We needed a plan, of some sort, about what to do in Nashville.

Throughout the journey, I used the credit card that my mom had given me whenever possible. I assumed she gave it to me so she could track my progress across the country. And I knew that, by using the credit card, she would know that I was all right. As a result, we still had plenty of cash on hand, so that wasn't an immediate concern.

But the money wouldn't last forever, and we needed to plan accordingly. Jobs, and a permanent living arrangement, would be a priority. The thing was, I had never had a job before; I had never needed one... before.

We entered the city at dusk; it felt familiar to me, yet different from my first visit here. I suppose Amanda had something to do with that feeling, but I was certainly a different person now. We checked into a hotel and decided that, in the morning, we would look for a more permanent living arrangement.

We went from place to place, looking for the right location. We did, eventually, find a little place that we could call home. Well, Amanda could call it home; I, on the other hand, had slightly higher expectations. A one-bedroom, one-bath apartment on the second floor, just somewhat better than what Amanda had in Las Vegas, was not what I would consider a home. A temporary solution to a long-term problem, but not the vistas, nor the spaciousness, of my youth. Certainly not what Amanda deserved, but this would be our reality... until I could figure out a way to rectify that situation.

It would be a few days before we could move in, so we decided to stay in the hotel while we set about looking for work. A completely new experience for me. I actually found a job in a record store. It seemed fitting to me. I mean, where else would a well-established asshole with extensive knowledge of music choose to work? Amanda found work as a waitress in a downtown country bar.

In the process, I found out that Waylon Jennings would be in town next week at Opryland. We had to be there, and Amanda could not talk me out of attending this concert. It was an extravagance, to be sure, but one that I could not miss.

From some sixteen rows back, we watched Waylon, and the band, perform. Amanda smiled, that exquisite smile of hers, as I sang the lyrics of 'Amanda' to her. I had never been so happy in my life; I had finally found what I had been looking for, unconditional love. Truth be told, I had found it once before, but not with the person that I had... wanted.

When I left work, I would go down to Amanda's bar. And all around me, I saw something that most people dismissed; I saw an opportunity. An opportunity that my dad would appreciate. An opportunity for me, and Amanda, to have a better life than a small, second-floor apartment in Nashville.

I spoke with Bill, the owner of the bar, often. I drank shots with him, played pool with him, and talked a lot about business. When I felt the timing was right, I made my move.

"So, Bill, you own this place, right?"

After taking a shot, Bill said, "Yeah, I own all the buildings on this block and the next."

I continued, "But this is the only one you are using right now, isn't it?"

Bill took another shot, "Yeah, I've had all of it for twenty years now, but this is the only building that's really usable."

I pressed on, "Yeah, I bet it would be expensive to renovate the rest."

Bill laughed, "More than they are worth."

I asked, "Why don't you just sell them?"

Pouring yet another shot, Bill replied, "I've thought about it from time to time."

Weeks of preparation were about to pay off, "What would you sell them for?"

Bill scratched his cheek, "I dunno, maybe one hundred fifty thousand for all of it."

Okay, I now had a price to work with, "Bill, that's too much... for this."

Bill leaned in, "Okay, Michael, what would you pay for it?"

I scratched my chin as if deep in thought, but here was my little secret that no one else knew, I had already done my research. The property, in its current state, was worth one-hundred thousand. The potential value, however, was much more. But one thing my dad had taught me when it came to business was never to pay fair market value for a piece of property. After, what I felt, was an adequate pause for reflection.

"Fifty, I might go as high as seventy-five."

Bill laughed, "I tell you what, Michael... I like you, so I'll make you a deal. You get me eighty thousand cash, and I'll sell it to you."

Bill held out his hand to seal the deal, and I shook it. I said, "I hope you don't take this the wrong way, Bill, but would you be willing to put that in writing for me?"

Bill laughed, "Sure thing, Michael."

Bill grabbed a cocktail napkin and a pen off the bar and then wrote out a bill of sale for me. I asked, "Could you please sign and date that?"

Bill laughed again, "Sure."

When he was done, Bill handed me the cocktail napkin. I shook Bill's hand again; I said, "Pleasure doing business with you."

And just like that, I had completed my first real estate deal. That night, when we finally made it back to the apartment, I presented my idea to Amanda. She asked, "What are you saying?"

I responded, "That my dad would know how to turn this place into something... *special*."

Amanda asked, "How?"

I said, "With money, time, and vision."

Amanda questioned, "Again, how?"

I replied, "This is what my dad does; he invests in real estate, repurposes it, and then he moves on with a handsome profit."

Amanda probed further, "What do you think your dad can do?"

I smiled, "I think that my dad can turn this into a mountain of cash for us."

Amanda continued, "How?"

Still smiling, "This is my deal; I would insist that he include you and me in that process."

Amanda said, "Okay? What do you need from me?"

A bit apprehensive, I said, "Nothing. But I do need to go home to present this idea to him."

Amanda asked, "What if he says no?"

I shook my head, "I don't see that happening."

After a minute of thought, Amanda said, "Then you go and let me know what he says."

I asked, "Don't you want to come with me? To meet my parents?"

Amanda stated, "No. If he says no, then we still need to have a source of income. If he says yes, then we will figure it out from there."

I protested, "But I want my parents to meet you."

Amanda said, "The last thing that I ever want to do is explain what I've been doing with you... to your parents."

So, I reluctantly agreed to Amanda's terms. I took just five hundred dollars cash, left her the rest, and then headed south from Nashville. Within a couple of days, I was pulling into a driveway I had not seen for more than six months. Not comfortable with just walking into the house, I knocked on the door. After a couple of minutes, my mom opened the door. She cried as she gave me a hug, "I knew that you would come back home."

I got choked up too. Who wouldn't under those circumstances? It felt like an eternity, but it was just a moment or two before she let go. My hair was longer, and I had a slight beard, but my eyes were just as blue.

Four Walls & A Roof

It felt good to be, once again, under these four walls and a roof. Life on the open road was not nearly as glamorous as one might think. The dust, and the many miles, take their toll on your body and soul. The days blurred together to form this long, chaotic chain of events that left you wanting to be someplace else, anyplace else but there, traveling on the road.

Ah, but my mom wanted to hear everything about my journey. As I suspected, she had followed my path, using the credit card charges as a guide. She wanted to know what I had actually done in the time since I left this place; she wanted to know what I had learned along the way. I was vague in my answers. I felt that it was best if I didn't give away too much information. Honestly, how do you explain nearly beating a man to death with a lead pipe in Kansas City to your mother? And I was still looking for an opportunity to introduce the idea of Amanda to my mom.

The questions would have to wait, as there was something that I desperately needed to do. I opened the door, stepped out onto the patio, closed my eyes, and listened to the ocean call my name. The sound of the surf, the smell of the salty air, the ocean breeze blowing through my hair; God was there at that moment, and She wanted to welcome me back to this place.

Thank you was all that I could say.

My dad was out of town on another business trip, and he wouldn't be home until the day after tomorrow. So, I had an early dinner with my mom and found myself with some time to kill; I called up my friends, and we headed out for another night of debauchery and reminiscence.

I regaled them with tales from the road, Nashville, Chicago, Las Vegas, San Francisco, Kansas City, and more. It was the truth, or my version of it, as I detailed the last six months and the change in my life. They asked questions, as expected, mostly about Amanda and what positions she preferred. The perverted nature of their questions aside, it felt good to be amongst true friends once again.

It was close to three when I finally made my journey back to the house. I stumbled through the front door and then instinctively made my way up to the bedroom. I passed out in bed as if nothing had ever happened and woke up in the morning questioning what I understood to be reality. It all felt like a dream, none of it could have ever happened, yet all of it was so real to me.

It was late morning as I made my way to the beach and worked my way out into the surf. It had been nearly seven months since I had attempted to catch a wave, and I found myself... lacking. I was better than this, but here I was late and missing so many waves. It felt like my heart was seven hundred miles away, wondering what Amanda was doing at this very moment. You cannot surf if your mind, and your heart, are not united as one. And, without a doubt, I was divided on this matter. I had wanted to be here, yet so much of me had wanted to be back in Nashville this morning with Amanda.

When my dad came home, we finally had that heart-to-heart conversation. I had explained my idea, and he was, of course, reluctant to pursue my vision.

He asked, "Why should I do that?"

I responded, "Why wouldn't you want to do that?"

Strictly business, he replied.

"I don't know that market, I'm not sure what opportunities exist, and I don't know if I can trust your opinion."

"Why not?"

"Because you've never offered one before," he replied flatly.

In a moment of truth, I conceded.

"I never wanted to be part of what you do, but this is an opportunity that I feel will never present itself again."

"Are you sure?"

"As sure as I am ever going to be," I nodded.

He said, "I'll look into it."

It took a couple of days, but my dad eventually agreed that I had recognized an opportunity. He had put just one condition on moving forward with this project; that I attend and graduate college with a four-year degree.

However, where I sought this degree was never a part of our agreement, so I thought that I would apply to Vanderbilt. As I prepared to return to Nashville, I received a phone call the day before my scheduled departure.

A familiar voice spoke flatly, "We need to talk."

The Devil You Know

The voice on the phone had invited me over to her house. I wanted no part of this drama, but reluctantly, I agreed. I pulled into the driveway and rang the doorbell. A familiar face greeted me: Kim.

"Hi, how are you?" she asked with a tone I couldn't place.

"I'm fine," I replied flatly. "What is it that you want?"

"Fair enough; I just wanted you to see something… before you left."

Not wanting to be there, I said, "Sure, what?"

She led me into the house and said, "There is something that I need to show you."

Uncomfortable, I asked, "Which is?"

"It's in the next room."

"Look, I liked you a lot, but there is somebody else that I love now."

"That's all right; I just wanted you to meet... your son."

Hearing those words, I felt like I was back in Kansas City, the vicious punch I saw coming but could not avoid.

"What?" I whispered; my head cloudy.

"This is your son."

I looked down at this little boy in a baby carrier as he looked up at me.

"No. that's not possible... you told me that you were on birth control."

"I lied."

I could feel the anger rising within me.

"Why the fuck would you do that?"

She flatly stated, "I wanted to make you happy."

Defiantly, I declared, "You made me happy without doing that."

"I wanted you to be happier. I never thought that this would happen."

My hands were up against my temples.

"So, you'd let me cum in you... to be happy? When I would have been just as happy pulling out and doing it *on* you?"

Frustrated, she spits out, "I don't expect you to understand."

"What's to understand? You're telling me that I'm a father, and I never wanted to be...a father."

Regaining some poise, she continued, "This is your son. Do you want to be a part of his life or not? That choice is entirely up to you."

The old me would have walked away from this situation. The new me, however, could not. I let out a sigh, "Are you sure that I am the father?"

"I last had sex three months before we did... and I haven't slept with anyone since you. So, yeah, I'm sure."

I looked down at the boy; he looked back up at me. There was something about that moment in time; something changes inside of you when you see your child for the very first time; it was frightening and yet so wondrous.

"What's his name?" I asked with a hoarse whisper.

She hesitated, for just a moment, before saying, "David."

Dumbfounded, I requested, "David? Did you name him after my brother? Why?"

"I know how much David meant to you. This boy means that much to me."

I shook my head in disbelief, "When was he born?"

"A couple of weeks ago," she stated. "November thirtieth."

Looking down at the boy, I inquired, "Can I—"

"Of course."

I reached down and picked up my son for the very first time. I started to cry as those baby blue eyes stared back at mine.

Once I regained my composure.

"What do you want?" I asked as I held those small blue eyes in front of me. "What do you need from me?"

"Do you want the truth? Or what am I willing to accept?"

I replied, "Both."

She responded, "First, I am willing to accept nothing from you. No money, no involvement, nothing at all from you."

Curious, I continued, "And the truth?"

"I don't care what you do, I don't care whom you fuck, but you belong to me now. First, and last, and always, mine."

"Are you saying that you want me to marry you?"

Kim said flatly: "Yes."

"You do understand that I love someone else?"

"Yes."

I continued, "I will cheat on you, with her, maybe with others... are you okay with that?"

"Yes," Kim responded, wiping away the tears from her eyes.

"Why on Earth would you accept these terms?"

She cried, "Because when I saw you in that club and wanted you for myself!"

I truly understood the concept of love, but how could anyone ever love me that much? I was just an asshole, flawed, and predisposed to fuck things up; how could anyone love that asshole?

Yet Kim was willing to let me be that asshole just to be with me. Amanda was still waiting in Nashville for my return, also willing to let me be that asshole just to be with me.

I never understood women, and I doubt that I ever would.

The Impossible Choice

Life is about choices. Who we are, whom we aspire to be, and who we will become; all of this revolves around the choices that we make. And now, I find myself at a literal crossroads, wondering which direction I should take. The implications of this moment cannot be exaggerated. Whatever decision that I make today will forever alter my life, tomorrow, and in the years that follow.

On the one hand, there is a girl that I genuinely like but do not truly love. She understands me and sincerely loves me despite my worst inclinations. She is the mother of my son, David. And that, alone, should be enough for me. It could be, but do I want more out of life than this direction might be able to provide?

On the other hand, there is a girl that I genuinely love but do not truly know. She understands me and sincerely loves me despite my worst inclinations. She might, one day, be the mother of my child. And that, alone, should be enough for me. It could be, but do I want more out of life than this direction might be able to provide?

Yes, we are the choices that we make. The real question is, can we live with these choices? For example, can I live with the choice that I am about to make? Better yet, am I willing to trust me with this choice?

Fear, regret, and uncertainty are powerful emotions that push us to run or fight. I could not decide if I should run to one or to the other. I could not decide which of my two desires I should fight.

Fear, the strongest of our emotions, consumes us; it paralyzes people as we try to make our way in this world. Am I afraid? Yes, but what, exactly? It is always the same fear; I am afraid of choosing the wrong path to follow. Either direction, honestly, is more than I deserve. I could not lose, but I could not choose because of fear.

Regret, while more subtle than fear, is just as dangerous. Absolutely nothing can crush your soul more than regret. In my young life, I have done a great many things that I regret. There are so many things that I would do differently now if given a choice. Even with these bad decisions behind me, what lies ahead, whatever my choice, will always be burdened by regret.

Uncertainty will always bring fear and regret sharply into focus. One could be so confident in their decision, but uncertainty would always find a way to make you question that choice. Two of the most insidious questions ever known to mankind are politely asked by uncertainty: Am I right? Or am I wrong?

So, if given a choice, what would you do? Live life with Kim, and my son, David or roll the dice with Amanda? Yeah, it's not so easy, is it? When you have to choose, simple things suddenly become a complex trap.

Fear, regret, and uncertainty take root and leave you wanting... clarity. Yet, clarity is no longer an option, is it?

In the end, I have to make a choice. I do not know what kind of father I will be, but I am afraid that I must find out.

David, I apologize, in advance, for all the things that I will fuck up along the way.

Kim, you will always deserve better than me.

And Amanda, my sweet love, I already regret this decision. And thanks to uncertainty, I will never know if I am right; or if I am wrong.

Hero of the Yesterday?

We are the choices that we make. Fuck you, Life, for making me choose; one path over the other.

THE END

Well, That Explains a Lot

As I turned the last page to the left, I thought to myself: *Well, that explains a lot.*

I had spent the last few hours in the mind of a complete stranger, yet someone that I had known my entire life. I shook my head and sighed, "That motherfucker."

I heard Traci ask, "What motherfucker?"

I had completely forgotten where I was and who might be around me. I looked up to see Traci sitting across the desk from me with a cup of coffee in her hand. I shook my head, "My Dad."

Traci looked concerned, "What about your dad?"

I lifted up the story and threw it in her direction, "Just when I thought I understood the bastard, he leaves me that."

Traci looked at the weathered pages, "The Story of a Young Heart…by Michael Taylor… your dad wrote this?"

I nodded.

"What's it about?"

I laughed, "The story of a young heart; the story of his young heart."

Knowing my passion for writing, Traci inquired, "Is it any good?"

I nodded, "Yeah, it is."

Traci looked at me, "Then why do you look so sad?"

"Because the motherfucker should have given me that when he was alive. Maybe then…"

Traci waited for me to continue, and when I did not, she questioned, "Maybe then, what?"

I sat there, silent, as I contemplated my response. My dad could be such a miserable bastard, and I never understood why. I always thought it was me; I always thought that he was disappointed in me. Now that I knew the truth, I would never have the chance to tell him how much I loved him. I just shook my head and began to cry.

Traci raced around the desk and hugged me. She whispered in my ear, "It's all right."

She kissed my cheek and then repeated her soothing words.

In between tears, I whimpered, "It's not all right."

"Maybe not today," Traci soothed. "But I promise you. It will be."

Traci held me tightly as I let thirty-plus years of emotion, fear, regret, and uncertainty escape my tortured soul. It was for only a few moments, but it felt like days. I had decades of unresolved feelings securely locked away, or so I thought. But once that seal was breached, there was no turning back the tide of emotions washing over me.

Eventually, I regained some composure. Wiping away the tears from my eyes, Traci kissed me again on the cheek.

"Hey, I love you. Look at me. I love you."

I looked deep into Traci's eyes, and, at that moment, I truly understood the impossible choice that my dad had to make all those years ago. Could I have been that strong? Could I really choose Stacey over Traci? Could I have made such a sacrifice? No, I don't think so. I would have rather died than make that choice.

Thirty-plus years of questioning what kind of man my dad was, only in death did I finally find the answer. Ironic, isn't it? My dad died a stronger man than I will ever be alive. Somehow, the thought of that reality gave me some comfort to me. I smiled as I tried to make peace with the demons in my heart.

Traci could tell that I was still conflicted, so she whispered in my ear, "What if I could make you forget about all of this?"

I laughed, "I don't see how."

Traci unzipped my shorts and exposed me to the world as she worked her way down to the nexus of my life. In ecstasy, my eyes rolled back into my head as she contacted her mouth. And, for a brief moment, I had forgotten about the death of my Father. I knew my mother had left the house a couple of hours ago. Apparently, I had forgotten the only other person who could still wander around this house. I was so close to finishing when I remembered; I had some help pulling me back to reality as Stacey walked into the room and smiled at me.

"Hey, Dad. How are you?" I had to laugh as the top of Traci's head hit the bottom of the desk. "What was that?"

I smiled, a guilty smile, as Traci emerged from underneath the desk. Traci said, "That was me. I went to grab a pencil for your dad."

Stacey asked, "So, where's the pencil?"

Traci looked at me, I looked at Stacey, and then Stacey said, "Oh my God, that is so gross! What the fuck?"

I interjected, "Hey, watch your language."

Stacey gawked.

"She was doing *that*, and you scold me for my language?"

"Wait, how do you know about *that*?" I interrogated.

Stacey looked at me, "I'm a teenage girl. I know way more than you think I do."

"Oh god, please tell me that you haven't."

Stacey smiled, "I'm not going to tell you anything."

Crushed by the thought of my little girl doing *that*, I said, "Then lie to me, please."

Stacey said, "Okay, Dad… I have never given a boy a blow job before."

Part of me was relieved, and part of me was *not* convinced. Then I had to ask, "But what about sex?"

Stacey said, "Yeah, you don't want to know about that either."

Oh God, this hurt almost as much as losing my father. My baby girl was becoming a woman, and there was nothing that I could do to change that reality.

"I love you but do not want to hear about your sex life."

"No problem," Stacey said whimsically. "And I'd prefer not to see yours!"

With a flip of her wrist, Stacey turned to walk away.

Hero of the Yesterday?

"I'll let you two get back to doing whatever you were doing before I rudely interrupted."

I looked at Traci, raised one eyebrow, and smiled.

Time to Reflect

Despite Traci's best efforts to distract me, I still needed to take some time and reflect on what I had just read. For more than thirty years, the foundation of my very existence had been predicated on certain facts. Facts such as the sun will rise in the East, the sky is blue on a sunny day, people that we love…die, and that my dad was an asshole.

Now, I would have to sift through what I thought to be facts and try to determine if any of it was actually fiction. The truth, as I knew it, was no longer a given; context and perception had twisted my sense of reality to reveal other… possibilities. It felt as if I were stuck in the famous Maurits Cornelis Escher lithograph '*Relativity,*' never knowing, with any certainty, which way was up or which way was down. What was it that my father wrote?

'Fear, the strongest of our emotions, consumes you; it paralyzes people as we try to make our way in this World. Regret, while more subtle than fear, is just as dangerous. Absolutely

nothing can crush your soul more than regret. Uncertainty will always bring fear and regret sharply into focus. Two of the most insidious questions ever known to mankind are politely asked by uncertainty: Am I right? Or am I wrong? Fear, regret, and uncertainty take root and leave you wanting... clarity. Yet, clarity is no longer an option, is it?'

It seemed to me that the abyss was overwhelming, the darkness below converged, with light from above, to form an eerie haze, and I was now uncertain of what to do next. Of all the things that life could take from you, perhaps the cruelest would be when it takes that sense of certainty away from you.

I found myself alone in my father's office, pondering the great mysteries of life and why any of this should mean something to me. Life and death were just two opposite sides of the same coin. The only difference is one you could see, and the other could only be experienced.

Earlier in this book, I stated that the average human being had just seventy-nine short years to write his or her story, and time was always ticking away from us as we navigated the complexities of life. Yet so many of us choose to ignore this simple truth; we seek out distractions to avoid confronting the unavoidable reality.

The pressures of life are enormous, and the weight of the world will eventually bring you to your knees. So, everyone, no matter how great or small, needs a diversion from time to time. Some people watch cat videos on the internet; some eat ice cream, and some watch TV. Yet others crave the temporary escape presented by drugs or alcohol. While it's true, I do love my whiskey. Writing is my passion; it is my attempt to make order out of the chaos swirling around me.

It's been almost three years now since I finished writing my first book. It was finally published two years ago, and it spent six months as a bestseller. In this day and age, that is considered a long time for a first-time author, or so they tell me.

Unfortunately, that book did not have the desired effect on people that I had hoped. Instead of bringing people together, which was my intent, it actually galvanized public opinion either for or against me. Somehow, by me sharing the intimate details of my life, I had managed to make myself more of a monster or a hero; it all really depended upon whom you asked.

And ask if I did. I spent a great deal of time online interacting with supporters and detractors as I tried to figure out where I went wrong. To my surprise, both sides said the same thing about my book; that it reinforced their opinion of me and society's general nature.

What?! How?!

Truth be told, the what and the how didn't really matter to me; people believe what they want to believe, despite the preponderance of facts that scream otherwise. What a strange world we live in, where the written word is given so much power over a select few.

So, I sought an explanation for why people would regard me in such opposite terms. Inevitably, I would get to the heart of the matter; what's the difference? Why would I be considered a monster by some and then a hero by others? Stunned silence, it always ended in stunned silence.

Some would sheepishly agree with my concerns, others would vehemently deny such a characterization, and still, many other people remained utterly silent. But they would all get back to the same point; either I don't like you and what you represent, or I do like you and what you represent. What, exactly, do I represent?

That was a tougher question for people to answer; it seems that I represent everything good and bad in this world. I'm not sure how that works or how that's even possible, but there can be no other explanation as to why I am celebrated or hated by so many people.

In the beginning, it truly bothered me; what people thought of me. Over the years, however, I've determined that it's just static - background noise – that's not important enough for me to care about. What is important to me, how I judge myself these days, comes from the people I love and the friends I respect.

Even before reading my father's manuscript, I had wanted to ask him: "If you could do it all over again, would you change anything?"

A few hours ago, I would have expected my dad to say, "Not a damn thing."

But now, I didn't know. And now, I would no longer have the chance to find out for myself. My Father did not make it to seventy-nine. He died more than twenty years before that mark because somebody thought that reading a text message was more important than driving a car. A wasted life, or so it would seem.

I lost the opportunity to have that discussion with my dad because I waited too long. Yeah, life could take just ten seconds to forever alter your reality; that was something that I knew all too well. Eight shots in ten seconds, that's what happened to me. And we all know how that ended up, don't we?

That experience and that choice were something that I had hoped no one would ever have to make again. People died due to my actions, and political fortunes were won or lost because of those random ten seconds in time. So, I somehow survived, while four others sacrificed everything in that process, and a fifth would never walk again. The burden of that truth never left me. Yet, here I was, still making excuses for my dad.

I hope my dad would have said, "I have never been whom I wanted to be, and I have never wanted to be who I am. But I am trying, and that, alone, should count for something in this world."

Yet, I never had the opportunity to give my father that chance, or to be more exact; I never took the time to give him that chance. If I did, would he have chosen a different path, or would he have done more not to fail so miserably as a parent? Would he be content with the knowledge that, in the end, I still loved him? Some answers, or so it seemed, were beyond the purview of mortal man.

So, when a man reeling in uncertainty could put the love of his Father above the endless possibilities of this life, for just a moment, time and space might open up to you as the tumblers click into place. And, in the blink of an eye, you could catch a glimpse of your true purpose within the universe. And when your eyes opened again, it was gone.

The Women of My Life

With all this conflict playing out in my mind, I felt like a nomad, without a drop of water to claim as my own, now completely lost and alone under the desert sun. I felt like a boat in distress, undulating on the waves, with no rudder or sails to steer me safely away from the jagged rocks ahead. The impending doom felt palpable as I attempted to navigate this uncharted path. Yet, that sense of dread put into sharp focus the need for me to address my own issues with the women of my life.

But where do I begin? *How* do I begin? After some contemplation, I decided it would be best to go from easiest to hardest. So, for those of you keeping score at home, that would put the lineup as Alice, Traci, Stacey, and then my mom. I would have *a lot* to discuss with my mom, and I don't think she would like what I say.

After reading my father's words, I now had many questions, and my mom clearly had been less than helpful with providing actual answers. It was obvious that she knew a lot more than she, up to this point, had shared with me. My biggest question was, why the sudden lack of candor? I mean, she had always been open and honest with everything else in my life, or so I had thought; yet why was the substance of my dad's life such a mystery? What exactly did Mom think that she should hide from me, and why?

Inquiring minds wanted to know now, but that would have to be the topic of discussion later today.

Right now, I bet some of you are asking, "What about Robyn? Why isn't she on the list?" Well, what about her? She wasn't exactly in my life right now, was she? And that was by choice, her choice, wasn't it? Robyn wasn't always available when I really needed her; she wasn't the bride that I had wanted at my wedding, and she wasn't there to comfort me when my dad passed. So then, why on Earth should she be on this list?

That sounded a little bitter, didn't it?

I honestly thought that I had dealt with this unpleasantness a long time ago, but evidently, I still held on to a vague resentment over the matter. I guess there's nothing like a little death in the family to dredge up unresolved feelings about the people in your life or those whom you wished were still a part of it.

Over the years, I had loved Robyn, and, at certain points, I had hated her too. Yet, for some reason, I had always needed Robyn to be a part of my life. I needed her today, but she had left me behind years ago. I understood why she had to go away, but that didn't make it any less painful for me. Not then, and especially not today. Life, however, did have a sense of irony; as that chapter in my life ended for me, thus another began.

So, I am sorry to say, Team RaD, that dream was now officially dead. Long live Team TaD!

With that decision, I had to think about what I might say to the four women who made the cut. Each woman posed a different challenge to me, each woman meant something different to me, and each woman held a different place in my heart. This was not going to be as easy as I had thought.

Knowing that each interaction would be different, I sat down with pen and paper in hand to write out bullet points of what I wanted to discuss. I separated the single page into a section for each woman, with their initial as the header of that column. I scribbled out random thoughts and soon realized that not everything would fit on one page. So, I shifted my approach and used a separate page for each of the women in my life. Who knew I had so much to say?

As I wrote down my thoughts, a clear pattern began to emerge. I hadn't been effective enough at communicating my appreciation, or any apprehension of the events in my life, to the women of my life. I found that I often left things, metaphorically speaking, unsaid. Worse yet, I found that I often assumed that these women would understand my true intentions.

I found that, of all the things that I had ever done, of all the things that I had ever said, it was never enough to convey the importance of these women in my life. And it wasn't as if I had really remained silent; no, I had said, and done, plenty over the years. Sometimes, I think, too much. But, at this point, I realized that it just was not enough. I found myself wanting to say more, to do more, for the women of my life.

I began to understand my desire for a long conversation with each of these women who meant so much to me. Each one of them, in their own way, had profoundly altered my life and had played an important role in determining who I was as a person. They helped me achieve more than I ever felt possible on my own, and now, each one would have to hear what I had to say. No filters, no assumptions, no boundaries, just the truth (or my version of it); God help us all!

A Guilty Delight

I picked up my phone, searched my contacts, and then dialed Alice's number. After a couple of rings, a familiar voice answered, "Hey, David. How are you feeling today?"

I responded, "Do you want the truth? Or would you prefer that I say what I think you should hear?"

Alice laughed, "The truth, always the truth."

I hesitated, "Alice, I really need to talk to you."

A bit more serious this time, Alice replied, "Of course, when?"

I sighed, "At your earliest convenience."

"Be at my office in an hour. I'll take you out to lunch. We can talk then."

And, although Alice couldn't see it on the other end of the phone, I smiled in relief, "I'll see you in an hour."

I informed Traci and Stacey that I had a meeting scheduled with Alice; I then handed her the keys to our rental car and told them that they should do lunch.

Traci asked, "Is Alice coming to pick you up?"

I shook my head, "No."

Puzzled, Traci inquired, "Then how are you going to get there?"

I kissed Traci on the forehead, "I'll take my dad's truck."

Traci wrinkled her nose just a bit, an involuntary twitch that I had noticed over the years. Near as I could tell, it basically meant Traci was confused by what she had just heard, seen, or read. It was just reason six hundred and seventy-four on my list of why I loved her. It's the little things, like an involuntary nose twitch, that make the difference in this game of life. Traci turned her head slightly to the side.

"Can you do that?"

I shrugged, "Who's going to stop me? My dad?"

She put her hand on my cheek, looked me square in the eyes, and smiled.

"Don't be a smart ass."

I smiled and quietly laughed, "I'll see you soon."

I kissed her cheek, turned, and headed for the garage. As expected, I saw my dad's truck waiting patiently for me. However, as I rounded the tailgate, heading for the driver's door, I stopped dead in my tracks. Something inside of me exploded as I made eye contact with that old familiar candy apple red nineteen sixty-six Mustang convertible.

"That's not supposed to be here," I said aloud as if anyone could actually hear me.

When I last talked to my dad, just a couple of days before his death, the Mustang was in the shop. I guess he got it back just in time for one last drive around town. I can't quite explain that sensation inside my heart, but I guess you could say that I was frozen with this feeling of guilty delight. It reminded me of my youth when I, quite literally, got caught with my hand in the cookie jar by my mom. I knew this car so well; it had always been a part of my life. But only today do I truly understand the importance of this vehicle, the true value of this treasure.

As a boy, I remember all those Saturday morning trips with Dad at the wheel, and me, in the passenger seat. I remember how much I loved to hear that engine growl as Dad shifted the gears. I remember looking up to the sky above as we rode around town with the top down.

Then a memory came back to me, a memory long lost amongst the minutia of everyday life. I remembered, I fucking remembered! I started crying again as the power of that moment actually made sense this time around.

I was probably ten, maybe eleven, when my dad asked me to get something out of the trunk. I was so excited as he tossed me the keys to fetch; I don't remember what. But I do remember that I emerged with this old jacket, and I asked my dad, "What's this?"

"That, my dear son, is the heart and soul of this car."

He walked to the back of the car, took the jacket from me, and hugged it. After a moment of reflection, my dad turned to me.

"David , this jacket must always stay in this car no matter what happens. Do you understand?"

I remember nodding at the time, but I had no idea what the Hell he was talking about; until this morning, that is.

Now, I have ridden in this car so many times in my youth, but I never had, once, ever driven it before. To the best of my knowledge, no one else had driven this car before; Hell, Mom wasn't even allowed to drive it. Ah, but I do know better now, don't I?

So, out of curiosity, I looked and found exactly what I was hoping to see: the key was actually there, sitting in the ignition. I snatched the key out of the ignition and headed for the trunk. With a certain amount of trepidation, I turned the key as the trunk popped open. I mean, the jacket still can't be there after all these years, right?

I smiled as I saw that old, familiar jacket was still in the trunk. A crazy thought took hold of my heart, does this jacket actually fit… me? Much to my surprise, it fit much better than I had ever anticipated. Giddy with excitement, I opened the driver's door. A torrent of lost memories washed over my soul, and a strange thought occurred to me; I needed to be a part of this legacy, for Uncle David, for my father, for all those Saturday morning trips that I remember sitting in the passenger seat as a kid.

I turned the key, and the car sprang to life; the engine responded with a growl every time I pressed the gas pedal. I laughed as the memories flooded my mind, and then I cried, knowing that this was all that I had left of my Father, those memories. I sat there for a few moments, not knowing what to do. I forced myself to put the car into first gear, pulled out of the driveway, and then headed for my appointment with Alice.

Seeing how it was such a beautiful day, I decided to take the scenic route; that is to say, I was going to be a little bit late. When I stopped at a light, I looked down at the radio to see an old cassette tape sticking out of the slot. I took the musical relic, inspected it, and then laughed, realizing this was the actual cassette tape #29 from my dad's book. As the light changed to green, I popped the cassette tape into the tape deck, and when the first song began to play, I hit the gas. The engine growled as I changed gears and sped down the road, racing toward my future.

Hello, Alice

It was just before one when I finally walked into the office. Debbie, Alice's receptionist, greeted me as I opened the door, "Good afternoon, Mr. Taylor. Alice is still in a meeting in the conference room. She said to please wait in her office."

Now, I had been in this office at least one hundred times before, and every single time Debbie had called me Mr. Taylor. And every single time that she called me Mr. Taylor, I would remind Debbie that she could call me David. I asked, already knowing the answer, "How many times do I have to say it? You can call me David."

Debbie replied, "At least one more time, Mr. Taylor."

I nodded as I let myself into the office. I sat down in one of the two leather chairs laid out before the big mahogany desk. I looked around to see various degrees and community awards spread out across the wall behind Alice's desk. In the middle of it was the article about me, Alice, and Traci leaving the courthouse on the day of the initial verdict. "Not Guilty" was the headline of the day. I wondered aloud, "Why is that there?"

"Because I wanted it to be there," Alice stated as she entered the room.

I got up from the chair and said, "Hello, Alice."

We hugged for a couple of minutes before Alice asked, "How about lunch at Kaity's?"

"I've never been there, but I heard it's very good."

Arm in arm, Alice and I left her office and walked the three blocks to the hottest Chinese restaurant in town. As expected, a line had formed for lunch, but Alice and I were waived to the front by the owner.

Someone in the line asked, "Why are they being seated before us?"

Kaity, the owner, said, "She owns the building, and she has a reservation."

I looked at Alice, curious about that statement. Alice smiled and then gave a little shake of her head to let me know otherwise.

The person stammered, "But... but... but you don't take reservations!"

Kaity shot back, "For certain people, I do."

We were seated in the back, away from most of the guests. It was noisy, but here, in this spot, we could talk. Although I had seen Alice at the funeral, it had been quite some time since we actually talked.

After some basic small talk, I said, "Alice, there's something that I want to say to you."

Alice laughed, "That's funny; there's something that I wanted to say to you."

I said, "Please, by all means."

Alice replied, "You first."

I put my hands up in surrender; there was just no use arguing with a determined and experienced trial lawyer. I requested, "Okay, but can I ask you a question first?"

Alice nodded, "Of course."

I leaned in just a bit closer, "It's a little personal."

Alice laughed, "Sure, ask away."

I scratched my chin as I posed my question. "Why did you become a criminal defense attorney?"

Alice leaned forward ever so slightly, "David, I'm going to tell you something that I have only told a handful of people before."

I nodded in acknowledgment. Alice continued, "I became a criminal defense attorney because my dad was arrested, and wrongfully convicted, of a crime when I was just fourteen."

I involuntarily sat back in the chair, "What?"

Alice leaned forward a little bit further, "Yeah, my father was wrongfully convicted of a bank robbery."

Now I leaned forward, "What happened?"

Alice took a sip of her jasmine tea, "My Father loved to fish; he went out to the St. John's River every chance that he got. A little boat, a little sun, a little time in solitude, he just loved the idea of fishing."

I nodded, "Yeah, my dad too…"

Alice continued, "But all that worked against him."

"How?"

She responded, "One day, while my dad was fishing alone, a bank was robbed in downtown Orlando."

I inquired, "Then what happened?"

"A photo of the robber was released to the press; my father was an exact match for the description. He was arrested and eventually convicted of the crime."

Thoroughly captivated by this exchange, I asked, "He couldn't have done it; he was fishing. Wasn't that a good enough alibi?"

Alice nervously shifted in her seat, "He couldn't prove it. No gas receipts, no credit card charges, no eyewitnesses, nothing that would put him forty miles away from the actual scene of the crime. The bank surveillance video, however, looked exactly like my dad."

Incredulous, I stated, "No fucking way!"

"I knew that he was innocent, but I just couldn't prove it in any court of law."

I asked, "So then what happened?"

Alice reacted, "I went to law school, trying to find a way to absolve my father of this crime."

"What happened next?"

Alice proudly stated, "I found the real perpetrator of the robbery."

"How?"

She answered, "By doing what the police did not do."

I responded, "What was that?"

"I expanded my search."

I implored, "How?"

"The lead Detective on the case truly believed my father's story," she continued. "So, he looked for other bank robberies in Florida that could be connected to this crime. He looked in Jacksonville, Tampa, and Miami but could not find a suspect who also was matched in the video.

"So, the Prosecutor decided that, since the video couldn't lie, and there were no other suspects, my father must have committed the crime. My father was charged and ultimately convicted of robbing that bank."

"How did you then find the actual bank robber?"

She asked, "Have you ever heard of Lake Placid, Florida?"

I thought for a moment, then I said, "Yeah, isn't that just a couple hours south of here?"

"It is. One Thomas Freeman robbed a bank in Lake Placid a week after the Orlando robbery. He was caught shortly thereafter and was, eventually, convicted in Highlands County for that robbery."

Not yet making the connection, I responded, "How did that help you?"

Alice retorted, "Thomas Freeman looked exactly like my father."

I sat back and put my hands to my face, "No fucking way!"

"With the help of the lead Detective, we were able to place Thomas Freeman in Orlando at the time of the robbery. The car he was driving matched the description of a car that was seen outside the bank, and thanks to advancements in DNA technology, we were able to prove that it was definitely Thomas Freeman, and not my father, who had robbed the bank in downtown Orlando that day."

In complete amazement, I asked, "How long did that process take?"

Alice shook her head, "Fourteen years. My Dad served fourteen years of a twenty-year sentence for a crime that he absolutely did not commit."

I took Alice's hand in mine, "I'm so sorry. How is your dad today?"

I could see the sadness in Alice's eyes as she answered, "He died two years later. But he died a free man, exonerated of that horrible crime."

"Why haven't you told me this before?"

Alice smiled, "I didn't want to burden you with my misfortune."

I responded, "I understand the professional limits on personal details, but you could have told me. I would certainly have been there for you."

"I know... but here's something that you didn't know."

Intrigued, I asked, "What?"

Alice replied, "When Traci called me about your situation, I originally said no."

"Why?"

She responded, "I don't defend murderers, rapists, or other violent criminals."

I rubbed my cheek, "Why is that?"

"I am very good at what I do, and I do not want to be responsible for successfully defending someone who might physically harm another person at some point in the future."

I nodded in agreement, "So then, why did you take my case?"

Alice laughed, "Because Traci said that she really liked you."

"I know, she told me. I still don't know why she remembered me from that football game."

Alice confessed, "But there's something more that you don't know."

"What's that?"

Alice continued, "Traci wanted you to have the best legal representation, so she offered to pay your bill."

I shook my head in disagreement, "If I had known about Traci paying my legal bill, I would have thrown your number away."

Alice put up her hand to stop me from talking, "I know, you were never supposed to know about that arrangement."

I ran my left hand up and across my forehead, "How much do I owe her?"

"Nothing; I couldn't take her money."

I put my hand over my heart, "Why would you do that?"

Alice looked up and a little to the left before she spoke, "You… you reminded me of someone. Someone who was very close to me."

And then it hit me like a lightning bolt, "Your dad… I reminded you of your dad?"

She nodded as she wiped away the tears from her cheek, "I couldn't help him when he needed it the most, but I could help you."

I shook my head in disbelief, "I had no idea."

"Funny how life places you where you need to be."

After lunch, Alice and I walked back to her office. As we were saying our goodbyes, she asked, "Didn't you have something that you wanted to tell me?"

I said, "With everything about your dad, I completely forgot. Yes, I do."

Curious, Alice requested, "Well, what was it?"

"All right, this is going to sound kind of strange, but… I wanted to tell you that… I love you, Alice."

She chuckled just a little bit, "Wow! Does Traci know?"

I shook my head, "No, no, not like *that*. I mean, like the sister that I never had."

"I knew what you meant. I love you too, David. Like the brother that I wish I had."

We hugged again and then finished our goodbyes. Alice headed back to her office, and I climbed back into the Mustang. It was still a beautiful day, so I decided to take the scenic route back to my parent's house.

What Say You, Traci Kaneko?

After lunch with Alice, I had several questions for Traci. The very first question was, how much was journalism, and how much was personal? Traci replied, "It was, at the very beginning, journalism. However, I let my personal feelings get in the way."

"So, I was just a story to you."

Defiantly, Traci replied, "No, you were always more than just a story to me."

I responded, "Why didn't you tell me about the deal you made with Alice?"

"How, exactly, do you tell a complete stranger that you have feelings for them? Or, at the very least, that you care enough to want them to be protected?"

Caught off guard by Traci's response, I countered, "I don't know, maybe by saying hey, I think that I might be in love with you."

She smiled, "Yeah, it would have been probably best to lead with that, but I had no idea how you would react."

I laughed, "Look at you and look at me. You are an intelligent person, one filled with compassion and a zest for life. You are everything that I wish to be; how could I not fall in love with you?"

"We each have our own insecurities."

I replied, "Maybe, but you are the most beautiful woman that I have ever met."

She responded, "Thank you for the compliment, but I respectfully disagree."

I answered, "Look, I don't know what happened to you before me, but I know this: I love you. And that is more than enough for me."

"I love you too, but my own insecurities created a monster. And I just don't see how I could slay that monster."

I laughed, "With love."

She smiled, "You are a magnificent bastard, aren't you?"

"Yes, yes, I am."

Traci smiled and kissed me on the cheek. We had, the two of us, reached an agreement. I would worship the ground that Traci walked on, and she would have sex with me. Who could ask for anything more?

Stacey Says

Having this conversation with my daughter proved to be harder than I had ever imagined. Eventually, I decided that we should head down to the park and sit on the benches overlooking the lake. Neutral ground, so to speak. As we walked, Stacey asked, "Are you okay?"

I smiled, "Yeah, I'm just thinking about things. Why do you ask?"

Stacey said, "You look conflicted, like you can't decide which way to go."

I replied, "Conflicted would be a good word for it. I'm just trying to process everything that has happened, you know?"

Stacey took my hand, "It's all right, I understand. I felt the same way after Mom's death."

I stopped, I tried to smile, but I could not. I simply stated, "I'm sorry."

Stacey asked, "For what?"

I wiped away the tears forming in my eyes, "For everything."

Stacey replied, "Hey, look at me. You have nothing to be sorry for."

I was crying now, "I wasn't there. I should have been there. I wanted to be… there."

Stacey was wiping away the tears for me, "You didn't know."

In a moment of complete honesty, I said, "God, I feel so guilty… for everything."

Stacey hugged me, "You're here now, Dad. That's all that matters to me."

I shook my head, "That's not good enough; you deserved better from me."

Stacey kissed my cheek, "She lied… to both of us. How can you feel guilty for something that you did not know about?"

I looked down at the sidewalk below my feet, "I just do."

Stacey lifted my chin up and looked me in the eyes, "Don't. Yeah, I lost my mother, but I found my father. A man whom I thought, for most of my life, was dead. How many people can say that?"

I was finally able to smile again, "Not many."

Stacey said, "You're God damn right!"

I replied, "Hey, watch the language!"

Stacey smiled at me, "Eff the language! I have my dad; what more do I need?"

I said, "Someday, you might not feel the same about that."

Stacey replied, "Maybe… maybe not, but today I do."

We hugged again as I whispered in Stacey's ear, "I love you."

She responded, "I love you too."

We continued our way to the park. We sat down on a bench overlooking the lake and then silence.

After a while, I asked, "Are you okay with Traci?"

She replied, "At first, no. I didn't see how you could love anyone but my mother. Eventually, I began to look at things in a different way."

"What changed for you?"

Stacey stated, "The way she looks at you. I can see how much she loves you."

Just the thought of Traci's love made me smile again.

"Yeah, I love her too."

She laughed, "That wasn't hard to see… you'd be a fool not to love her."

I looked at Stacey, "I understand that there are so many things going on in your life…things that you would not want to share with me. I hope that you feel comfortable enough to confide in Traci. She does love you, you know that, right?"

"If she loves you, then she has to love me. We are, after all, a family."

Mom's in the Kitchen with a Glass of Wine

It would be nearly six when my mom finally returned to the house. Upon seeing her, I said that we needed to talk. I could tell that she was trying to avoid the discussion that had to happen. Yet, I finally cornered her in the kitchen as she poured herself a glass of wine. I began my investigation by asking, "Did you read Dad's book?"

She replied, "No, I never did."

I asked, "Do you know what he wrote?"

"I have a pretty good idea… but no."

I stated, "You know that he said you only told him about me… *after* I was born."

"That's true."

I started doing the math in my head, "Wait, I was told that you and Dad married a year before I was born. That's not possible then, is it?"

My Mom tried to explain, "The month and day are correct; we just moved back the year by two."

I shook my head in disbelief, "Why would you do that?"

"He left before you were born. In those days, we had no way to share important information without making a phone call. Your dad left before I could make that phone call."

I said, "And when he was gone?"

She confessed, "I tried… but I had no idea where he went. His Mom didn't know either."

I asked, "And when you finally told him?"

"He held you in his arms and cried. A couple of days later, he officially asked me to marry him."

Changing the subject, I asked, "Who is Amanda Jones?"

Surprised, my mom answered, "At one time, she was your dad's business partner in Nashville. Why?"

I slammed my hand down on the counter, "She's in the book, Mom! She *is* the book!"

A Stranger Approaches

As the melee in the kitchen continued, a stranger approached the front door and pressed the doorbell. Awaiting the pizza that I had ordered nearly an hour ago, Stacey jumped up and shouted, "I'll get it!"

Fully expecting to see and smell the deliciousness that is pizza, Stacey swung open the door and said, "It's about damn…"

This was *not* the pizza delivery guy. Stacey instinctively retreated behind the front door, "Can I help you?"

The stranger spoke, "Is David here?"

Stacey had, more or less, gotten accustomed to strangers asking to speak to me. Most were harmless enough, but some were a bit unstable. This person looked more like the former than the latter, but you can never tell. Stacey knew what to do, "David? David, who?"

"David Alan Taylor, your father, Stacey."

Panic set in, and Stacey froze.

Right at that moment, Traci rounded the corner to ask what was taking so long when she locked eyes with the stranger, and her demeanor immediately changed, "Can I help you?"

The stranger replied, "I need to speak with David."

Traci asked, "Why?"

The stranger said, "It's of a personal nature. It won't take long; I just need to give him this envelope."

"I'll take it from you; I'm his wife."

The stranger continued, "I have to give it to him in person."

Traci examined the stranger closely, seeing no warning signs of someone looking to harm any of us. Traci, without breaking eye contact with the stranger, said, "Stacey, go get your dad."

Stacey walked into the kitchen and interrupted a heated exchange between my mother and me.

"Dad, there's someone at the front door."

"If it's the pizza guy, I've already paid."

Stacey shook her head, "No, it's not the pizza guy. It's someone else."

I bit my lip in frustration, "Can they come back or something? I'm in the middle of this—"

"They said it's a personal matter. They have an envelope that they need to give you."

I sighed, "All right, I'll be right there."

Stacey turned and left the room. I looked over at my mom.

"This isn't over yet. We'll get back to this soon enough."

I walked over to the front door and asked, "Can I help you?"

"David, it's so good to finally see you."

Confused, I inquired, "Do I know you?"

The stranger replied, "No, we've never met before."

Tired of this dance around the purpose of this unannounced visit, I demanded, "Who are you?"

The stranger held out her hand as she spoke, "Mr. Taylor, my name is Isabella Castillo Martinez, and I have been personally instructed by your uncle, David Alan Taylor, to present you with this envelope."

"My Uncle died before I was born."

Isabella smiled, "No, Mr. Taylor, your Uncle David is alive and well. And he, very much, looks forward to meeting you and your family."

To be continued…

Special Acknowledgements

Where do I even begin? So many years ago, I set out on this journey with an audacious destination in mind: to become a published author. Oh, there were detours, dead ends, potholes, flattened armadillos on the side of the road, and failed relationships littered throughout this meandering expedition. Once, I even thought that I had found a place I could call home forever; but it wasn't meant to last. No, it seemed that I was destined to be out on the open road, with the top down, radio blaring, and headed for the distant horizon under a bright blue sky.

Of course, I need to thank the usual suspects in my life for making this possible: my wife, my family, Terry & Jill, Paul & Lisa, TAZ, and Sir Paul McCartney.

Yet, there are some additional people that I also need to acknowledge for their support. Thanks to VM and Loob, my CKA (or CQA, depending entirely upon your preferred spelling) brothers, for all the mayhem and fun that we've had over these many years. Mitch, you really need to watch out for that first step, it's impossible to see in the dark, and we don't want a repeat of Halloween night. To Robin, your *Emmy* means more to me than it does you; I find that refreshing with all that's happening in this world. And thanks to my Editor Beverly, you made my book better by breaking my heart with all your red pen edits.

Finally, thanks to Mike Score, Ali Score, Frank Maudsley, and Paul Reynolds for writing, recording, and releasing the 1984 album "The Story of a Young Heart"; the inspiration for this book.

In music, we find a purpose for telling the stories we tell.

I hope you enjoyed this tale; it's the reason that I wanted to be a writer when I grew up. All these years wasted, or so it seemed, and then *it* happened.

—Henry D. Trett

2023

About the Author

Henry D. Trett is an American author, artist, and entrepreneur. In addition, Mr. Trett has the unique honor of being the oldest of three children, and, oddly enough, also the youngest of five.

Curious how that works, huh?

An Orlando native, Mr. Trett currently resides in the Southeastern region of the United States with his wife, three dogs, eighteen koi fish, and a tortoise named Lucky.

Coming Soon by Henry D. Trett

HERO OF TOMORROW?

www.ingramcontent.com/pod-product-compliance
Lightning Source LLC
Chambersburg PA
CBHW072013190726
48293CB00001B/263